The Invisible Foe

(a novel)

Iris Graham

Three
Towers
Press

Milwaukee, Wisconsin

Published by
Three Towers Press
An imprint of HenschelHAUS Publishing, Inc.
www.henschelhausbooks.com

ISBN: 978159598-859-1
E-ISBN: 978159598-860-7
LCCN: 2021940588

Cover art by Arianna Eisendrath

Printed in the United States of America.

ACKNOWLEDGMENTS

This book is dedicated to the loving memory of my son Walter, my only child, who, although he left this world way too soon, loving thoughts of him continue to inspire me in many ways. There is no greater love than that of a parent for a child

I also pay homage to my parents for my remembrance of them—the good and challenging times that we had, living a simple but joyful life—remains etched within me and are reflected in this work.

I wish to acknowledge my dear niece, Yvonne, for all her encouragement through the process of this work. She has stood firmly by me when, at times, I felt like giving up.

Finally, I want to thank Arianna Eisendrath for her steadfastness in creating the cover art which set the tone and mood for the book.

For all these, I am profoundly grateful.

—Iris Graham

CHAPTER 1

The quiet that pervaded the afternoon was suddenly shattered by the angry barking of the dogs. Someone screamed, and I rushed to the window to see what had caused the disturbance. Halfway down the path leading to our house was the figure of a woman running for dear life with our three dogs fast on her heels. She made it to the gate and pulled it shut just in the nick of time with the angry animals taking giant leaps at the structure in their futile attempts to get to her. The huge Alsatian dogs with their tan color and black saddles, looked all the more menacing with their fangs bared.

"Hold de dog, hold de dog!" the woman screamed in a terrified voice. It was then that I recognized her as one of our neighbors.

I started to giggle at the ludicrous scene, but quickly checked myself when my mother appeared beside me.

"What's goin' on out here?" she asked, her voice filled with anxiety, and as she took in the scene, gasped. "Oh, my God!"

She called a stern command to the dogs as she rushed out to the front porch. They either did not hear or deliberately chose to ignore her, for they did not pause in their determination to keep our unexpected visitor out.

1

"Down, down!" Mama shouted, stamping her foot hard on the tiles. "Come here at once!"

The dogs reduced their barks to low, ominous growls. They turned reluctantly and moved slowly toward their mistress with heads lowered and tails wagging. They kept sneaking backward glances at their intended victim, who did not even attempt to move.

"It's all right," Mama called as soon as the dogs were close to her. "You can come on up; they won't bother you now."

She had obviously spoken too soon, for in swift contradiction of her statement, all three dogs moved as one, taking short, menacing steps forward the minute Mrs. Bowen nervously slipped the latch on the gate. Their behavior was totally out of character. Once they had challenged the right of anyone to be on our property, and be assured by any member of the family that it was all right, they would invariably settle down without paying further attention to the caller. For some inexplicable reason, which had me greatly puzzled, they seemed bent on keeping this woman out.

I watched, fascinated, devilishly hoping that Mrs. Bowen would give up and go away, but she seemed determined to gain entry. At that point, I moved slowly out onto the porch and stood behind my mother, who then solicited my aid in quieting the dogs.

I accomplished this with some difficulty which added to the strangeness of the situation because of all

the family except my father, I had a special way with the dogs and they were always quick to obey me. Now it took a lot of prodding for them to follow me to the backyard. They did not take kindly to being leashed, and I hated having to confine them, especially since the visitor was someone for whom I harbored an intense dislike.

When I returned, the scene was unchanged. Mama just looked at me and I nodded, whereupon she signaled to Mrs. Bowen to enter. The woman slowly opened the gate, took a few cautious steps inside, paused uncertainly, then made a mad dash up the path. I was unable to contain myself then and the laughter bubbled forth, to be quickly suppressed when I caught Mama's stern look, which could not quite conceal her own smile.

"Sorry about the dogs," Mama apologized when Mrs. Bowen arrived panting on the porch in front of us. "They don't usually behave like that."

"Ah was never so frighten' in me life," Mrs. Bowen said between gasps, "Ah think Ah better si' down. Ah'd never like to go through anyt'ing like dat again."

Mama led her into the drawing room where it was cooler. Mrs. Bowen plunked herself down on the settee, drew a large handkerchief from her bosom, and wiped her sweaty face with a trembling hand. I almost felt sorry for her.

"Can I get you anything?" my mother asked with deep concern, "A cool drink would help."

"Yes, thank you."

Mama started towards the kitchen, but I was already ahead of her. I poured a tall glass of limeade from a large earthenware jug that Mama always kept filled at a shaded corner on the kitchen counter to keep cool, and hurried back to the drawing room.

"Here me come on a goodwill mission," Mrs. Bowen said between sips of her drink. "An' Ah could'a lose me life."

Such exaggeration, I thought.

"A goodwill mission?" Mama asked somewhat skeptically.

"Yes, me dear," Mrs. Bowen lowered her voice, exuding an air of mystery. "Sometimes dere's t'ings we should know, an' because we don't know dem, we not able to save we'self from a whole lot of unpleasantness."

"What do you mean?" Mama was cautious.

"Well," Mrs. Bowen lowered her voice even more. "You know people see t'ings an' dey talk, but de one who should know always in de dark."

"Yes?" Mama prompted. She looked around and saw me lingering at the door, her eyes spoke a message, and I immediately left the room.

I was furious. *Why shouldn't I be allowed to sit and listen to what the woman had to say?*

I was no longer a little girl. After all I was nineteen years old, which made me an adult, and I had every right to be treated as such. I went to the

4

adjoining room, where I lingered. I could hear the murmur of their voices but that was all.

When I could no longer bear the suspense, I walked casually out the back door and around to the front porch where I sat hoping to catch a word or two that would enlighten me as to the purpose of the visit, but here I had no better luck.

Suddenly the voices inside grew louder. I sat still hoping at last I would learn something, but I barely had time to vacate my seat and leave the porch before Mrs. Bowen walked out, accompanied by my mother. By this time, I was outside bent over, pretending interest in a bed of yellow gladiolus that grew in thick clusters by the steps. I was afraid to meet my mother's eyes, because I felt certain that she knew exactly what I was about. I remained as I was until the discomfort of my posture forced me to straighten up. My timing could not have been worse.

At that precise moment, Mrs. Bowen came abreast of me, and I watched in horror as she reached out a callused hand and patted me on the head. I cringed inside and hoped that would be all, but I had to suffer the indignity of having my cheeks pinched, caught between thumb and forefinger, and shaken. I felt the uncomfortable stretch of my lips as she completed the ritual.

"Yu so pwetty," she said using baby talk which further irritated me. *Horrible woman*, I thought, with enough venom running amok in my mind to shrivel her, if only she knew it.

I never understood why she always felt compelled to treat me in the same manner whenever we happened to meet, ever since I was a little girl. As I grew older, I had devised ways to escape her and they had worked until now. I had difficulty keeping the scowl from my face, for I knew my mother was still watching me. I forced a smile for her sake and quickly moved away.

I was idly sitting in the kitchen still nursing my resentment when Mama returned from accompanying Mrs. Bowen to the gate. She did not say a word as she went about getting things ready for dinner. When I was no longer able to restrain myself, I burst out angrily.

"I can't stan' that woman. I wish she wouldn't come here."

"That woman?" my mother queried with raised brows, "I know no one by that name, Adelene."

That was, of course, her way of telling me that my form of address was not at all acceptable to her.

"That Mrs. Bowen," I said, reluctant to give in all the way. "She's a horrible old woman."

Mama did not respond right away, and when she did, her tone was reproachful.

"That's not a nice thing to say. There's no benefit in saying unkind things about another person."

"But I don't think she's a nice person at all, Mama. She's always touching an' pinching me with her dirty ol' hand," I grumbled.

"Well, touching you sure doesn't make her a bad person," Mama said patiently. "It's a bad habit, yes, I'll admit that, but instead of harboring all that ill feeling, it would be better to tell her how you feel should it happen again."

"I'll tell her alright, and she's not going to like it." I was still feeling angry.

Mama stopped what she was doing and with arms akimbo looked fixedly at me.

"Adelene, I want you to understan' something." She did not raise her voice, but each word was uttered with such quiet authority that I quailed. "I will have no child of mine, regardless of age, being disrespectful to anyone, no matter what position they hold in life. Always leave your path clear wherever your steps may take you so that you can look every person straight in the eye without fear. You understand?"

"Yes, ma'am," I felt humbled.

"Good. Now just get that look off your face and give me a hand here."

My mother was never a long-winded person. Whatever she had to say would be delivered in as few words as possible with such profound wisdom and understanding that it remained etched in my consciousness forever. I did not fully appreciate it all then, but later in life, I was to draw from her teachings, and profit greatly from them, not only within myself, but also in sharing with others.

At the dinner table that evening, my curiosity was aroused. My mother, though taciturn by nature, seemed to have retreated even further within herself to the extent that she hardly noticed what was happening around her.

"Something wrong, Liz.?" my father asked, finally.

"No," she replied, looking around the table just in time to see Paul sneak something from Andy's plate. Mama pulled herself together, then gave Paul one of her unblinking "no-nonsense" stares until he returned what he had taken.

Later that night, for the first time in my life, I heard my parents arguing. Mama's voice was slightly raised. She sounded angry. My father's responses were less emotional. I held my breath while I listened. I very badly wanted to sneak closer to their room to hear what was being said, but I knew what the consequences would be if I were caught eavesdropping.

My parents never displayed much affection in our presence. They would sometimes give each other a peck on the cheek, or Father would sometimes slip an arm around Mama's waist and give her a little squeeze. It always fascinated me to see the look of pleasure on her face, and I knew beyond a shadow of a doubt that she loved him very much.

Later, after their voices had died down, I went thoughtfully to bed, but I could not fall asleep. I lay wide awake long into the night thinking of this new development. Uppermost in my thoughts was the strange meeting between my mother and Mrs. Bowen earlier that day. I was convinced that there was some connection. Suddenly I felt a twinge of fear as the thought took hold, and I wondered what would happen next.

I was to remember that day for a long time after and wondered if the dogs had sensed something sinister about our visitor, and if they had succeeded in scaring her off, whether or not events would have taken a different turn.

CHAPTER 2

The next morning, I got out of bed earlier than usual. It was my job to feed the chickens, and I thought the sooner I got that out of the way, the sooner I would get to the breakfast table before my father. I wanted to see both of my parents together.

When I got back to the house, Mama was busy cooking salted cod fish and ackee (our Jamaican national dish) in that quick, efficient way she did everything. Served with fried dumplings, it made a very delicious meal and was everybody's favorite. My interest in food that day was far less important than seeing how my mother looked. She seemed the same as usual, but one couldn't always tell.

"How come you're up so early?" she looked searchingly at me.

"I couldn't sleep anymore," I said. I had difficulty meeting her eyes.

"Why?"

"I dunno," I looked away and quickly added, "I come to help you."

"Well, get to it then. You can set the table," she said.

I busied myself but all the time I was aching to ask the question that was uppermost in my mind. I knew, though, just what her answer would be, because we were raised with the firm understanding that whatever transpired between adults was definitely not the concern of children. Right or wrong, that's the way it was.

Later in the day, Mama left on some mysterious mission. She looked grim. Whatever it was had to be very important since she never left home except on Sundays or on special social occasions.

My older sister, Phyllis, and I did the shopping, for having to take care of the family and help run the farm, Mama had her hands full at all times. My father, on the other hand, spent most of his time on field inspection tours for the branch of government service for which he worked. The rest was given to the farm and his social activities.

Mama returned home much sooner than I'd anticipated. She still had that tight-lipped look. She went straight to her room, closed the door and for a long time, there was only silence.

When she emerged, she seemed herself again. I watched her closely and kept hoping that she would confide in me.

Father got home earlier than usual that evening and he used the time to do some long-neglected work in the backyard. Everything seemed normal, and I began to relax. It is said that appearances can be deceiving, and I realized just how much truth there was in that statement when once again, I heard my parents arguing that night. This time, I threw caution to the wind and sneaked closer to their room.

"You had no right to do anything like that!" Father sounded angry.

"I had every right in the world," Mama responded in kind "I will not be a laughingstock in this town. I've always trusted you, and I expect you to live up to that trust."

"You listen to too much gossip."

"Wrong. It's the other way 'round," Mama's voice had a quality in it that I'd never heard before. "I don't listen enough. If I did, I'd know before now what was happening under my very nose."

"What's happening, Liz?" Father sounded less angry. "You jus' tell me what you think is happening?

"Look, I want it stopped right now, you understand? Because I'll not tolerate it."

"You're making a mountain out of a molehill."

"So, that's how you see it?'

"That's exactly how I see it," Father said shortly. "What you got to complain about anyway?"

"You never have enough time to spend in your own home. You hardly know your children. You're like a stranger to them. I've got to bear the burden of everything."

"I suppose you fo'get that I have to work to support all of you?"

"That's always your excuse," Mama snapped, "but I hope when you receive as you give, you won't complain."

"What do you mean by that?" Father demanded.

"Time will tell," Mama said.

"I can tell you one thing, Liz," Father said in his normal tone, "if you're going to start nagging me after all these years, it's not going to do you any good, so jus' continue to be your ol' sweet self because I really don't know where the hell you get all them wild ideas."

I was shocked to hear my father use such a word to Mama. In my disturbed state of mind, I thought I detected, somewhere in that statement and the way it was delivered, some kind of threat. What Mama's response would have been was lost to me when I was interrupted.

I turned guiltily to meet Phyl's disapproving look. I had been so engrossed with what was happening behind that closed door that I didn't hear her come in.

"Shhh." I put a finger to my lips and tiptoed away from the door. "They're quarreling."

"You're crazy" She looked suspiciously at me.

"It's true." I grabbed her arm and pulled her along to her room. "Something's going on."

"You had no right to go snooping outside their door. You ought to be ashamed of yourself."

"Phyl, I know. Don't keep on about it," I said impatiently. "You want to know what I think?"

"No, I don't," she said with finality. "Your imagination is always running away with you. What is not your business, leave alone."

"Oh, you're too prim and proper," I shot at her as I left her room.

The night seemed endless. My mind remained alert, speculating on the probable cause of the sudden conflict between my parents. If only Phyl had let me talk it over with her.

It was about a week later before I plucked up enough courage to approach Mama on the subject. I probably wouldn't have had the nerve except for the circumstances. We were both in the drawing-room at the time. Mama was doing some darning while I leafed idly through the day's newspaper. Suddenly, she started reminiscing on her childhood days, and I had the distinct impression that there was a longing for things that had passed. It was during a pause that I asked the question. She looked steadily at me for a while and assured me, quite calmly, that it was nothing serious and that I should forget about it.

I felt so frustrated I wanted to scream. Why couldn't she acknowledge that I was no longer a child and she should stop treating me as one? I restrained myself, however, pulled the paper up to cover my face and pretended to read and to hide the fact that I was fuming inside.

"That's strange," Mama's voice broke through the silence that had ensued.

"What's strange, ma'am?" My curiosity got the better of me. She was looking towards the door with a puzzled expression on her face.

"I thought I saw something but...," she broke off. A frown creased her brows as she asked, "Adelene, where are the dogs?"

"They're in the backyard, why?"

"Are they still chained?"

"Yes, ma'am."

"That explains it then."

"Explains what?"

"That a stray dog was able to come in."

"That's what you saw?"

"Well, yes, at least I think so." She still seemed puzzled. "The dogs didn't even bark."

I got up and went outside. I looked around as far as I could see but there was no sign of a canine intruder.

At the time of the incident with Mrs. Bowen, it had been unanimously decided that the dogs would be kept leashed during the daytime so as to avert possible tragedy in the event someone else thought fit to ignore the large warning sign posted on our front gate. We did not want trouble. The dogs were watchdogs, for our protection only. Father had insisted on keeping all three to discourage any attempt at praedial larceny, which caused the small farmers in the area considerable annual loss of crops.

Our farm was located in the district of Benin in the Parish of Saint Ann, some twenty-five miles from the resort town of Ocho Rios on the Island of Jamaica in the West Indies. The land was rich and fruitful with rolling hills and lush pastures.

I released the dogs. They showed their gratitude by frisking all about, wagging their heavy tails almost knocking me over. I hated having to keep them chained, but I comforted myself with the thought that they were free to roam at nights. They followed me back to the house and settled themselves at various vantage points on the porch.

"Did you manage to get it out?" Mama asked, after I had seated myself.

"What, ma'am?"

"That little dog."

"Oh, I didn't see any dog."

"You know it wouldn't stand a chance if those three got to it," Mama said with some concern.

"Well, if there was one, it must've found its way out again or it may be hiding somewhere." I tried to reassure her.

"I'll ask your father to check the fence to see if there is a break somewhere big enough for animals to crawl through. I have enough to worry about without having to worry about them as well."

She picked up a sock, looked at it dubiously, decided it wasn't worth darning and dropped it back into the little basket. I resumed my perusal of the paper. Mama always relied on me to give her every little detail of the news since she never took time to read anymore.

Daylight had begun to fade, and the air was alive with the sounds of nocturnal creatures. I got up, put the light on, and took a quick look outside before closing the door. I was halfway back to my seat when I was arrested by the most frightening, rattling sound. It was as if the windows were being ripped from their frames. It lasted for just a few seconds but it left us badly shaken.

"My God, what's that?" Mama gasped.

"I don't know," I said in hushed tones. "Maybe something fell."

"Oh, no, that didn't sound like something falling."

Just then we were joined by my younger siblings. Paul, Andy, and Janet, who came running into the room, full of questions we couldn't answer.

"Paul, let's go and see," I said moving towards the door.

"No!" Mama said sharply. "Don't go out there. You don't know what you may run into."

The noise had awakened to dogs and they had set up a loud barking. We heard heavy footsteps running down the walkway with the dogs in angry pursuit.

"It mus' be a thief," Paul said.

"Could be," I said, "but he met his match."

"Adelene, check the doors to see if they're all locked," Mama said.

I complied, not letting on how afraid I was to move through the house all alone. As I left the kitchen, I felt a prickly sensation in my back as if I were being

17

watched I comforted myself with the thought that it was only fear, and hurried back to join the others.

We didn't know it then, but that was the beginning of a series of mysterious happenings that would become part of our daily lives for days to come.

CHAPTER 3

Two days later, Mama complained that she was not feeling well. I insisted that she take a rest, and I was very surprised when she complied without protest. It was not like her, and it made me think that in all the years she had spent taking care of her family, I had never once heard her complain. The only times I could recall seeing her in bed in the daytime was after giving birth to a child.

I attributed Mama's feelings to tiredness and refrained from giving any serious thought to it. I had to finish fixing the meal she had started so I was kept fully occupied. My sister, Phyllis, got home from work a bit early that day and was surprised not to find Mama bustling about as usual. I explained the reason why.

"Boy, she must be dying," Phyl said flippantly.

"Don't say that!" I said sharply.

"Why, you know I'm just joking."

"That's nothing to joke about," I snapped.

"Well, for heaven's sake!" She eyed me as if she thought I'd gone crazy, shrugged her shoulders, and went to her room.

I went immediately to Mama's room and knocked. When there was no answer, I tiptoed in to find her sound asleep. I looked at her a moment and wondered why it had scared me so when Phyl had jestingly referred to death in relation to her. My mother and I were very close. The same could not be said of my father. He was a strict disciplinarian. He laid down the rules and we were never allowed to get out of line. As I was about to leave the room, Mama woke up.

"That you, Adelene?" she asked.

" Yes, ma'am," I said "You feeling any better?"

"Not much," she struggled to a sitting position. "I can't understand why I should feel this way."

"Maybe you should stay in bed."

"No!" she said emphatically. "I hate to lie in bed when I'm not sick."

I didn't argue with her but watched as she slowly swung her legs off the bed. She stood dizzily before pulling herself together: I held on to her as we walked back to the kitchen.

Mama said hardly anything throughout dinner. It was as if she was somewhere else, which had me worrying all over again. Immediately after, she returned to her room. I exchanged looks with Phyl and noticed that she too had a concerned look on her face.

"You think something's wrong," I stated rather than asked.

"Must be," Phyl said, knitting her brows. "That kind of behavior is not at all like our mother."

"Perhaps all the years of hard work are catching up with her," I said somewhat hopefully.

"Maybe," Phyl sounded doubtful "I think I'll take her temperature before I go to bed."

"Good idea," I said.

I got Paul and Andy to do the dishes. They expressed their displeasure but I ignored them because in our home, it was expected that each one should contribute to its upkeep.

I dried and stored the dishes while Phyl tidied the dining room. Phyl looked like Father, with a round face and high cheekbones. In contrast to me, she was smaller and had soft hands that she hated to get dirty. How appropriate for her profession as a nurse. So far, I was the only one who was truly domesticated, and I loved it. I was taller with a sturdy build and strong hands, and everyone said I favored my mother. To me, Mama was beautiful, with an oval-shaped face, soft black hair, and warm brown eyes.

James, our older brother, became a teacher. He was married and living not far from home. It will be interesting to see what our younger siblings end up choosing as their life's work. Me? Strange as it may seem, my desire is to take up farming. I loved the land and derived immense pleasure from planting things and watching them grow.

Later, Phyl informed me that Mama's temperature was normal. I relaxed then. There obviously was nothing to worry about.

Since my father did not work on a set schedule, he seldom had dinner with us, but Mama would always sit with him while he ate, and they would talk and make their plans then.

When Mama did not reappear, I set the table in the customary fashion and waited for Father's arrival. He was later than usual or so it seemed because of my unaccustomed role. I began to get drowsy but before I could fall asleep, a frightened cry shocked me to full consciousness. It came from my mother's room. I rushed to see what it was all about.

"Get that animal out of here!" she said indignantly as I entered the room. "How could you all sit there and let it come in?"

"What animal, ma'am?" I asked rather confused.

"That little dog, the one that was on the porch the other day."

"Mama, there's no dog here," I said patiently. "You must've been dreaming."

"I'm not dreaming," she said emphatically. "Don't you contradict me, child. It's standing right there." She pointed towards the foot of the bed and a puzzled frown creased her brow.

"Well, it was there," she said defensively.

I refrained from saying anything. There had to be a logical explanation. Mama was too rational to succumb to wild imaginings. To appease her, I began looking into corners and under the bed. I was still engaged in my fruitless search when Phyl came into the room.

"What's going on?"

I told her. She thought it was very funny.

"Mama, you know how real dreams can seem at times," she said laughingly as she felt Mama's forehead.

"All right, have it your way," Mama said, then pointedly changed the subject. "Did your father come in yet?"

"No," I said, "but don't worry, I have everything under control."

"Good." She sounded so tired. "I'll be up in a little while."

"Mama, please rest," Phyl said firmly. "We can take care of things. You've done enough."

"It's not the same," Mama said.

"Whether or not, you can do just so much," Phyl was determined that she should stay in bed. "Father won't die if you can't wait on him for once."

Mama didn't reply. Phyl winked at me, and I smiled halfheartedly. I felt very uneasy but kept it to myself. It was bad enough seeing Mama lying in bed, but for her to be hallucinating as well seemed too much of a coincidence.

Phyl must have sensed something in my manner, for as we left the room, she tried to reassure me by saying she didn't think there was anything seriously wrong with Mama that a few days rest wouldn't cure. I wanted to talk with her some more but she didn't linger.

Knowing that she had an early shift at the hospital the next day, I didn't try to detain her.

Not wanting to be alone, I went to my brothers' room, hoping that we could while away some time by engaging in some kind of game, but they were both sound asleep. The books from which they had been studying were still clutched in their hands.

I guess I should have been more discreet but I was so full of my assumed responsibility that I got a little carried away, so instead of leaving them alone, I woke them up.

It wasn't an easy task, however. Andy remained in a kind of daze but Paul was so furious I thought I'd have to run for my life.

"Why don't you change your clothes and go to bed," I said.

"You wake a man fah that?" he asked crossly.

"Mama would wake you," I said defensively.

"Well, you're not Mama," he grumbled.

"And you don't care how she feels." I realized immediately that it was an unfair remark and totally uncalled for, but I couldn't take it back.

"I bet you're the only one who care," he said sarcastically.

"Look, I'm sorry," It was my place to back down. There was no sense to a prolonged bickering that could only destroy what I was trying to accomplish.

"You know she's not feeling well."

"Yes, but that don't mean you have to boss me' 'round" He sat up on the side of his bed and gave me a hostile stare. "So why don't you get out an' let a man change?"

I spun on my heels and headed for the door.

"What's wrong with Mama, anyway?" he asked.

"I don't know. She's just not feeling well," I said, then added, "She's in bed."

There was an abnormal stillness in the house. It was scary. I fervently wished that Father would come home. As I moved towards the living room, I was once again overcome by that prickly sensation at the nape of my neck, and with it an overwhelming sense of fear.

I thought to go and check on Mama. Just then, a slight sound behind me made me turn quickly, my heart pounding. It was Paul. I was about to give him a piece of my mind when there came a loud crash and the sound of shattered glass followed by a rattling noise. Paul clutched at my arm, and we both stood too petrified to speak. Mama called then, and we ran to her room, holding on to each other.

"What was that noise ?" she asked.

"It's probably the kitchen window," I said. "Remember that loose pane? The breeze must've knocked it out."

"I really don't know what's happening 'round here." She groaned as she got out of bed.

She looked at my brother and me in a rather dazed way, then asked about the rest of the family.

"They're in bed," I said.

"I'd better go and see if they're all right."

"Why wouldn't they be all right, ma'am?" I tried not to let on how disturbed I really was.

"I don't know, but I'm not taking any chance," she said.

Paul and I stuck closely to her as she walked slowly through the house, checking all the doors and windows, which were securely locked and intact. I had thought that the racket was loud enough to wake the dead, yet it had failed to rouse Phyl.

Mama told Paul to go to bed. He protested, saying that if someone was trying to get into our home, he was our only defense. He had very definite ideas of what his actions would be and went on to demonstrate his moves. Mama smiled indulgently but made no comment.

It was then that I first began to question in my mind the hours that my father kept. Why was his job, which primarily had to be accomplished during the day, keep him so late out at nights. As my thoughts wandered through forbidden channels, it suddenly struck me that there was something terribly wrong about the atmosphere. My anxiety intensified as certain possibilities of what may have occurred outside claimed my full attention.

CHAPTER 4

I don't know how long afterwards, maybe ten minutes or so, before I heard the dogs. I only know I felt an overwhelming sense of relief that I almost shouted for joy. Moments later, there was the turn of the key in the lock and my father entered the room. He showed surprise at seeing the three of us sitting there.

"What's going on here?" he asked in that stern tone of his.

"I don't know, Berty," Mama replied. "But whatever this strange thing is, some stop will have to be put to it."

"Put to what?" he asked, looking puzzled.

"Whoever or whatever is trying to frighten us out of the house."

"You're not making any sense, Liz."

"You remember that incident I told you about with the windows?"

"Yes?"

"Well, the same thing happened again just a little while ago, only it was worse."

"Oh, nonsense. What could it be but the breeze?" he sounded amused. "The windows are probably loose."

"It's more than that!" Mama was adamant. "There is no possibility that the windows could all of a sudden be that loose. Besides, I doubt whether there was any breeze."

"So, what'd you think it is?" he eyed Mama suspiciously.

"It's unnatural. That's all I can say."

"Oh, come now, Liz." Father's tone was laden with disapproval. "Don't tell me you're getting superstitious. You know how I feel about that. Didn't you tell me that you all heard someone running that first time?"

"It probably was a duppy," I quipped.

"Now, I don't want to hear any such fool talk in this house." He gave me a stern look.

"Sorry," I said, abashed.

"There's probably a simple explanation and we'll find it soon enough."

"It better be soon," Mama said.

"Why don't you children go to bed," he said. "And Liz, you don't look too bright yourself."

"I've not been feeling well all day. In fact, I was in bed till the disturbance."

"Then you'd better go back to bed. Come on."

Father took her gently by the arm to help her up from the chair. He seemed genuinely concerned, and I felt guilty about the thoughts I'd harbored during his absence. My brother did as we were told, but I lingered. I wasn't about to let Mama worry about getting his meal on the table.

I watched as she stood up, wavered, and would have fallen had Father not held her. She hung limp in his arms. He picked her up easily and carried her to their bedroom. I followed close behind. My heart was thumping so hard I could hear it.

"Oh, Lord," Mama groaned after he'd gently laid her on the bed, "I'm burning up."

Father pressed the back of his hand against her forehead, moved it towards her temple and under her chin. He looked puzzled.

"Do you think she's got a fever, sir?" I asked him.

He shook his head. His brows furrowed. "I don't understand it."

Mama seemed to be trying to get her clothes off as she shifted uncomfortably from side to side.

"Your sister home?" Father asked me.

"Yes, sir."

"Go get her."

"She's sleeping."

"Doesn't matter. Go and wake her!" he said impatiently.

I had difficulty getting Phyl awake, which explained how she had managed to sleep through all the commotion.

Once again, Mama's temperature was normal. However, as a precaution, Phyl gave her two Phensics and we stayed with her until she fell asleep. On our way out, Phyl suggested that it would be wise to have Mama see a doctor as soon as possible. Father agreed, and on that note we retired for the night.

The next morning, when I went to check on Mama, to my surprise, I found her room empty. I walked into the kitchen and she was already there.

"You should've stayed in bed," I scolded.

"Well I feel a lot better," she said. "Besides, I wanted my early morning cup of coffee."

"That's no excuse," I responded. "I could've got it for you."

"But you just got up," she pointed out.

She did look better but I had this incredible guilty feeling that I'd somehow let her down.

Mama looked at me and smiled.

"I never see a child worry so much," she said, patting me lightly on the head. "Come on, cheer up. I'll be fine."

Feeling somewhat reassured, I got busy with the morning's routine. Father and Phyl were always the last ones to have breakfast. During that brief period alone with Mama, I took the opportunity to inquire, as casually as I could, about her seeing a doctor.

"Doctor?" She sounded surprised. "Why should I see a doctor?"

"Because of what happened last night."

"Oh, that!" She was thoughtful for a while. "I don't need a doctor for that."

"But Mama, people just don't faint for no reason?"

"Maybe not, but I'm alright now."

"Well, perhaps Father will take you anyway," I said hopefully, knowing Mama, nothing short of a bulldozer could make her move an inch if she didn't want to.

Throughout the day, I kept a close watch on her without making it too obvious. I finally admitted to myself that I was worrying unnecessarily, that is, until my overactive imagination began working overtime, and I became obsessed with one thought. I was utterly convinced that my suspicion was right when, later in the afternoon, Mama again went to her room to rest.

Phyl laughed outright when I confided in her.

"I think I'm right," I said, reluctant to let go of the idea.

"You're forgetting that Mama is over fifty," Phyl said. "She'd be crazy to let anything like that happen."

"Well," I shrugged. "It's possible."

"Yes, it's possible, but it would be very unwise."

I didn't realize till then how much I was hoping that Phyl would agree with me, and that my suspicion was true.

"It would be kinda nice to have a baby in the house again, though," I mused.

"Honestly, sometimes I wonder 'bout you," She eyed me as if she thought I'd gone mad.

"Why don't you hurry up and get married so that you can have some babies?" I teased.

"Girl, I have no intention of burdening myself with a whole lot of children. One would be enough, two the most."

"What about Alan?"

"I don't know. We never discuss it. Besides, I would never let him force me to do anything I didn't want to." She paused thoughtfully. "Truth is, sometimes I'm not sure if I want to really settle down with him after all."

"Why not?" I was surprised. "I thought you two had a good thing going."

"Well, yes, but that's not everything," she sighed. "It's just that being a housewife doesn't appeal to me very much. I don't think it's in me to wait hand and foot on any man. Cooking his food, darning his socks, and washing his clothes. Ugh!"

"But both of you have your work. I'm sure you'd be getting someone to do most of that for you," I pointed out.

"That's true," she said, without much enthusiasm. "We'll see. Right now, I have to get some sleep. I have to be up very early in the morning."

She stretched out on her bed and closed her eyes. I stood looking at her for a few seconds and left without further comment. We all respected Phyl's need regarding her rest. We knew it was essential to her performance because her job was a taxing one.

That evening, Mama stayed up as usual. She never went to bed until everyone had done their homework. It was very important to her that her children got a good education, especially since she had been denied one herself through a series of family misfortunes during her youth. She had felt the loss deeply and was determined to make sure that the same thing did not happen to us. Of course, I was the exception and perhaps, her only disappointment.

As the evening wore on, I noticed that although Mama seemed to be functioning normally, she still looked peaked. I convinced myself that with a good night's sleep she would be back to her old self again and everything would be back to normal.

It turned out, however, that they were feelings to which I had given premature expression. The next morning, she did not get out of bed at all.

My parents were early risers. Usually, while my mother tended the kitchen, my father would be out looking after our domestic animals, milking the cows or goats, so we would always have fresh milk in the mornings.

The kitchen was empty when I got there and nothing was done. I quickly filled the large, old enamel kettle and set it on to boil before I hurried to my parents' room and knocked.

"Come." It was my mother, but her voice sounded so weak. She was lying there—so still.

She looked up at me when I reached the bed.

"Oh, it's you, Adelene."

"Yes, ma'am. You feeling sick again?"

"I feel so weak." Her voice was just above a whisper. "Don't know what's wrong with me."

I felt helpless. I didn't know what to say.

"Adelene," It seemed an effort for her to speak.

"Yes, ma'am?"

"See what you can do 'bout breakfast; the children have to go to school. Go now."

Under the circumstances, there was nothing I could do but comply. So I went back to the kitchen and hurriedly made a pot of oatmeal porridge. I was cutting slices from a loaf of hard-dough bread when my father returned with a foaming bucket of milk. He placed it on the table and went off to wash without saying a word.

By the time he returned, I had placed a steaming bowl of oatmeal and some bread with homemade butter that Mama had churned by simply putting the rich cream in a jar and shaking it until the butter rose on top. It was very light and delicious. I knew he wouldn't like it, but it was the best I could do in the time I had. He made a face and, murmuring, took a few spoonfuls of oatmeal before pushing it aside.

He was buttering bread when I put his coffee on the table. It was very strong with lots of cream and just a pinch of salt, the way he liked it.

There was still no verbal exchange between us. I, for one, did not know what to say. It was not until he had finished eating that he cleared his throat rather noisily and said, "I don't know what's suddenly happened to your mother, so I'm going to see if I can get the doctor to come and see her today."

I felt relieved. At last, I thought, he was taking a positive step. Before I could respond, however, the rest of the family trouped in, all dressed for school. They were all surprised not to find Mama there and wanted to know where she was.

"Your mother isn't feeling well today," Father said. He got up to leave and stood looking at each of them in turn. I felt uncomfortable. I badly wanted to say something, but was unable to get the words out. My father always had that effect on me. The truth is, I was always a little afraid of his gruffness, being the sensitive person I was. Finally, he looked directly at me.

I quickly averted my eyes.

"Adelene."

"Yes, sir?"

"Unfortunately, I have to go to work, but I'm relying on you to try and get your mother out of bed and help her to get dressed if possible. No good for her to give way to her feelings"

"Yes, sir." I resented his remark. I knew my mother and he, of all people, should know her even more. Mama was not a "bed" person.

"The rest of you see that you do what you have to do and don't give your mother any trouble."

"Yes, sir," the little ones replied in unison.

He left and I filled a cup with coffee and hurried to my mother's room. She was in the same position. She didn't appear to have stirred at all. I thought it rather odd, if not abnormal.

She refused the coffee, and I was unable to persuade her to drink it. I'd try again later, I thought, and reluctantly returned to the kitchen.

"Adelene," Janet said plaintively. "You goin' comb my hair for me?"

"You finish your breakfast?"

"Yes, all of it," She sounded tearful. "I'm goin' to be late."

"Come on, then," Back in the room we shared, I quickly plaited her hair and tied in her ribbons.

Andy was shouting to her to hurry.

Paul had taken the opportunity to see Mama. I met him on his way out, a worried look on his face.

"Why she look like that, Adelene?" he asked in a whisper.

"I don't know," I replied in kind, not wanting to worry the others.

"I think something strange goin' on. I don't feel like goin' to school today," he said unhappily.

"No!" I said sharply." You go to school. You know how Mama would feel about that. Staying home won't help anything."

"Alright," he said.

Some things are easier said than done. Trying to get my mother out of bed proved an impossible task. She wouldn't budge; she asked repeatedly to be left alone. After a while, I decided there was no point in continuing to pressure her, so I smoothed out her sheets, got everything nice and neat in the room, and went back to the kitchen.

This was going to be a long, hard day, but it was up to me to keep things going.

Around mid-morning, I was surprised and pleased to hear sounds of movement coming from my parents' room, as if Mama was moving things around. Curious, I dropped what I was doing and with a wide grin on my face, tiptoed toward the bedroom door. As I approached, something fell with a loud crash. *That vase on her dressing table*, I thought. *Too bad.* It was a very old porcelain piece and Mama cherished it.

I peeked into the room and froze. The smile wiped from my face. Mama was still in bed, apparently sound asleep as evidenced by the steady rise and fall of her chest. The room was intact. Nothing had been disturbed.

CHAPTER 5

I stood rooted to the spot, too scared to move. My mother and I were the only ones in the house. I was sure of it, yet there was no denying what I'd heard, and no amount of rationalizing would alter the fact.

I steeled myself and walked slowly into the room towards the bed, my head felt as if it had grown twice its size. I took a few deep breaths to try and alleviate my fear. As I stood by the bed, I felt a cool puff of air and the sensation as if something had brushed quickly by me. I shook Mama. I had to get her awake. I had to! This way, there would be two of us. I prayed that the day would end so my brothers and sisters would be home.

Mama woke up, and a sixth sense told me to try and keep her awake. I got another pillow and managed to prop her up. In the meantime, I kept up a flow of aimless chatter. She looked at me and smiled.

"What you trying to do now?" she asked in a weak voice.

"Trying to keep you awake," I said "I think you're sleeping too much."

"I have nothin' else to do," she said.

"I'm goin' to help you get up. You can't give up like this."

I pulled the sheets back.

"No, no, Chile. I'm too weak," she protested.

"You'll feel stronger if you get out the bed," I insisted. "You can sit in the drawing room where I can see you better."

"Why you have to see me?"

"I don't know." I couldn't tell her my fears. "Jus' feel that I have to. Please, Mama, please."

She looked searchingly at me for a long time. Something in my tone must have touched her.

"Alright," she said at last. "Help me up."

With an arm around her waist, we went at a slow pace to the drawing room, where I seated her in her favorite chair. I rushed back to her room to get a shawl she always wore if she had to go out on a rare cool evening, and wrapped it around her shoulders. She smiled her thanks, and I, feeling encouraged, went back to my work in the kitchen.

In between tasks, I'd walk the few steps that allowed me to check on her unobserved. Most times she'd be sitting back with her eyes closed or just staring into space. It was uncanny. That was not my mother.

At three o'clock in the afternoon, Doctor Anderson arrived accompanied by my father.

I was never so happy to see anyone in my life. Now we would have an idea as to what the problem was.

Father assisted Mama back to the bedroom with the doctor in tow. Waiting for the result of the examination proved almost unbearable. It seemed like hours. It was difficult for me to carry on with my work, so I let everything go and hung around waiting for the doctor to emerge.

When he did, instead of setting my fears at rest, he only managed to increase them because the good doctor said he could find nothing physically wrong with Mama. and she should, in fact, be up and about.

"She's probably just tired," he went on to say. "You know, having to take care of a large family for so many years can take its toll. All I can suggest is that she continue to rest for a few more days, and she should be as good as new."

I looked at my father; his face was as inscrutable as ever. It would have been good to know what his thoughts were on the diagnosis. To me, it made no sense, none at all. Another opinion seemed called for at this point.

Father accompanied the doctor back to his car. On his return, I plucked up the courage to ask him what he thought. He took his time answering.

"Doctor Anderson is known to be a good doctor," he said thoughtfully, "but I'm wondering if he missed something. Your mother has always been a strong woman. I can't understan' how she jus' collapse like this."

"Maybe you should try another doctor, sir?"

He shook his head in bewilderment.

"We'll see," he said. "We'll jus' wait and see."

I felt dissatisfied, but before I could say anything further, we were interrupted by the return of my siblings from school.

Paul dropped his books on the kitchen table and immediately went in to see Mama. I wondered if he had accomplished anything much in school that day. There were anxious questions from the others before they, too, went in to see her.

The night passed without further incidents except for Mama's moaning at intervals. My father, for once, had decided to stay home that night, and his presence made us all feel more secure.

Katherine, our helper, came the next day. She had been in and out of our home for as long as I could remember, helping my mother twice each week with the washing and ironing.

She was just learning of Mama's illness and asked at once to see her.

I accompanied her to the bedroom and we both stood silently looking at the diminutive figure lying on the bed. Mama was wide awake but seemed unaware of our presence. Her gaze focused at a point at the foot of her bed, an act that I found quite scary.

My heart was full of compassion, and as the hot tears gushed up to settle on my lids, Katherine touched me lightly on the arm and motioned me to follow her outside.

"How long since Miss Liz sick?" she asked, her brows knitted. "She was aw'right when I lef' her las' week."

"She took sick Friday."

"Dat's five days today." she said thoughtfully. "How come nobody let me know?"

"Well," I sighed. "It's jus' that nobody's thinking clearly right now with all the strange things happening 'round here"

"Like wat so?" she eyed me with interest.

I hesitated, feeling embarrassed. It was hard to guess how anyone would take the truth, and I had a deep fear of being ridiculed. However, I managed to give her a brief outline of my experiences of the past few days and waited for her reaction.

"Humph," she snorted. "She see a doctor yet?"

"Yes."

"So wat him sey wrong?"

I explained.

"Rubbish!" Katherine snapped. "Miss Liz strong as a horse."

"Bu...but Katherine, you see how she is," I protested.

"Yes, Ah see, but wat Ah want fe know is, if is bline oono bline or is fool oono fool?"

"What you mean?" I was taken aback.

"Look, it don't tek no scientist to see wat is happenin' to you modder. It's as clear as daylight," she said emphatically. "Dere's nothin' natural 'bout it."

"You not making sense," I said.

"Yes, Ah makin' sense, but is fah you to understan'." She gave me a look I could not define.

"See what?" I was vainly trying not to let my thoughts wander in the direction I suspected she was pointing.

"Well, den, you want me spell it out fah you? Or you tink if you preten' it wi' go 'way?"

"What?" I was feeling resentful of the tone she was taking with me.

"Dat Miss Liz dyin' jus' as sure as me name is Katherine."

"No!" I gasped, horrified by the bluntness of her statement. "Don't say that!"

"Well, honey," Katherine continued in the same manner. "You can't hide from de truth, so de sooner you face it, de sooner you can get help for yur modder."

I stared at her. Everything flashed through my mind at once. Stories long told of mysterious deaths and even more mysterious causes. Miraculous cures of unknown maladies affected by strange people. My father's scorn of anyone who would be so illiterate and superstitious as to harbor thoughts of anything outside the norm. My own fleeting thoughts that I had quelled in the past. Now I wasn't so sure. Now I'd have to face them.

"You...you mean... *obeah?*" I was even afraid to say the word.

"Well," Katherine sighed. "She wake up at las'."

"Oh, God!" My hands began to tremble as I became engrossed with this new possibility.

I felt as if my heart was being crushed.

"You really think so, Katherine?"

"Certain as Ah can be."

I placed my hands on my head, grabbed handfuls of hair, sank slowly on a step and moaned, rocking back and forth.

My behavior must have irritated Katherine, for the next thing I knew, she was shaking me roughly by the shoulder.

"You stop dat right now, because if you even cry a bucketful, it won't help Miss Liz in her present condition. You have to seek help fah her."

"I don't know what to do," I said between sobs. "The doctor..."

"Doctor!" Katherine scoffed. "Wat dem know?" Then went on to answer her own question. "Ongly wat dem learn from book an' such an' dat can't help everybody. First t'ing to know is you might ha'fe tek her out de house."

"Katherine, you crazy? How you expect me to do something like that?"

"Well, you jus' gwine have to fine a way if need be."

"Father would never agree to it."

"Girl, wake up," Katherine sounded cross. "Yur father don't have to know a t'ing. When him gone to work, how him gwine know wat happenin' here?"

"He'll kill me," I protested.

Well," she remarked dryly. "Maybe some t'ngs wort' dyin' fa. You t'ink 'bout dat, Now Ah have work to do."

In desperation I rushed back to my mother's bedside. Could Katherine be right? I was in a quandary. I couldn't get the thought of possible witchcraft from my mind. The more I thought about it, the more plausible it seemed. As the day wore on, I became obsessed with it.

Everything else had become secondary to my concern for Mama. The problem was to try and convince someone else. The possibility of that was as remote as trying to reach up and touch the moon.

Katherine said nothing more to me on the subject for the rest of the day. But before she left, she went once again to look in on Mama. On her way out, she told me that if I needed her, I would know where to find her. At the door, she paused and said rather gravely, "Adelene, don't wait too long or it might be too late."

I could find no words to reply, but as the door closed, I knew without a doubt exactly what I was going to do. But first, I'd have to have a talk with my older sister.

I waited up that night until very late. Phyl did not come home, which led to the obvious conclusion that she had decided to work through the night. This meant that my talk with her would have to be postponed for another day since she would be in no condition to participate in anything on her return.

I began to seriously consider taking things in my own hands regardless of the consequences. It turned out to be another sleepless night for me, weighing the pros and cons.

Twice, I had to rush to comfort my mother after hearing her agonized cries. After my second visit to her, all my doubts fled, and I felt a calm determination to try whatever means necessary to seek a cure for her.

"'Don't wait too long," Katherine had warned.

My God! What amount of time would be too long? I fell asleep thinking that even a few hours could probably be too long.

CHAPTER 6

I t had reached the point where everyone, with the exception of my father and Phyl, dreaded the coming of night. We would make certain that everything outside was taken care of before dark. The dogs released. The windows and doors locked and bolted. There was still no answer to the phenomenon that haunted us daily.

My father, being the eternal skeptic, scoffed at our fears. He could not understand just what we were talking about because whatever it was always happened some time before he arrived home. To appease us, he had reinforced the doors and windows and tested them, but nothing worked. Our nocturnal visitor still managed to accomplish the impossible.

At first, I didn't associate the two things, and perhaps no one else did, but it gradually dawned on me that there was a definite link between my mother's illness and the mystery that surrounded us. I was afraid to voice my suspicions to other members of the family for fear of being ridiculed. Yet, despite all our efforts, Mama's condition worsened.

We'd tried just about everything. Our Aunt Rose, my mother's older sister, who had extensive knowledge of various indigenous herbs and their properties, was known to have effected cures that had been medically

classified incurable. She had learned the skill from her
father, who had been a self-taught herbalist. Aunt
Rose made a lucrative living brewing and selling her
"tonic," as she chose to refer to her concoctions.

There were whispers that she was in fact an
"obeah woman," and people who did not know the
truth, stood in awe of her. Aunt Rose was well aware of
the rumors but she went smilingly about her business.

"People always condemn wat dey don't understan',"
she said to us one day when Mama repeated a deroga-
tory remark that she'd overheard concerning her. "If
dey feel happy to go on sayin' tings 'bout me den let
'em. I know de truth 'bout myself, an' dat's what
count."

I acknowledged the wisdom of her philosophy, but
couldn't understand how she could be reconciled with
the meanness of her accusers.

Aunt Rose had cooked up a batch of her famous
"tonic" and had taken it to us to give to Mama. She
said that even if it did no good, it certainly would do no
harm. So each day I gave Mama a small portion, and at
times, she seemed to perk up some. She also began
eating better although she still showed no interest in
what went on around her. We felt encouraged until one
day I heard her yelling.

"Adelene, take it away!" she cried. "Take it away!"

I rushed into the room, my heart in my throat.

"What, ma'am?" I asked, scared out of my wits.

"The food!" she said. "Why did you bring me such a big plate of meat? I don't want it. Please take it away!"

I was aghast. All I could do was stare at her.

"Take it away!" she said urgently.

I don't know what made me go through the motion. It appeased her, and she lay quietly with her eyes closed. After a while, she spoke again.

"Adelene, please bring me some water, I'm so hot."

"Yes, ma'am."

As I hurried out, I kept glancing back over my shoulder with every step I took. Was my mother going crazy? It was a thought that I had tried to avoid pursuing before. It was true that so far, she had not shown any sign of violence, but she was hallucinating more frequently. She took a few sips of the water and immediately lapsed into a lethargic state.

Another day slipped away and things remained in the same precarious manner. We watched helplessly and waited. The minister from our church came to visit, and subsequently a group from the Prayer Ministry was sent to pray with us. Since we were informed beforehand, my father had endeavored to take time off from work to be there. I'd not seen him showing any real concern for Mama. But then, Father was like that. Except for the times he got really angry, he always managed to mask his feelings with an expressionless face.

Most times that day as I moved in and out of Mama's room, I could see her eyes following me.

"Why you putting all those chairs in here?" she asked in a drained voice.

"The people from the church comin' today," I reminded her.

"Oh, yes." She took a deep breath then closed her eyes. "I hope they won't stay too long. I'm too tired."

"We'll take care of that. Don't worry," I promised while I smoothed out her cover.

She seemed to have fallen asleep again. I couldn't tell without disturbing her so I went quietly out of the room. There was this enormous ache in my heart that was getting worse every day. I could not understand how a seemingly healthy woman could succumb to an unknown malady and be reduced to just a shadow of herself in so short a time. I had difficulty associating my mother with the rapidly deteriorating figure lying in that bedroom. There had to be a way to help her. I knew I intended to try whatever the cost.

I told my father what Mama had said, and he promised to have the meeting as brief as possible. I left him and went to the kitchen to prepare some refreshments while he admitted the guests. There was a large tin of freshly baked potato pudding, from which I proceeded to cut slices and put them on plates in readiness for serving, while I brewed coffee and set water on to boil for tea in case there was a matter of preference. I didn't wish to join the group. I couldn't.

It would have been too emotional for me, but from my vantage point, however, I could clearly hear everything that went on. As was customary, a hymn, appropriate for the occasion, was sung very softly. Then each person said a prayer. I counted five. How many people there actually were, I didn't know because Father had admitted them.

When there was a longer pause than usual, I thought that it was all over when a voice rose with deep emotion, beseeching the heavenly Father to lay his healing hands on the beloved sister and restore her to health.

It all sounded so different from all that had gone on before. Something about the tone of voice began to annoy me. It sounded so insincere. I began to hope that each word uttered would be the last, but it went on and on, and with it my annoyance grew. I was curious to see who was putting on such a grand performance so I walked to the bedroom door and peeked in.

I was taken aback when I discovered that the voice was that of a Mrs. Elliston, a woman who had recently moved with her husband and daughter to the district. No one knew where she hailed from and she remained a mystery. How she could be a part of this group was a puzzle to me. I couldn't recall ever seeing her in church.

I studied her for a while. She was very attractive, probably in her late thirties. She was always well groomed, with a haughty bearing that clearly indicated that she considered herself better than everyone else. In fact, I could not fathom how she could be married to a man so different from herself in appearance. The gossips had it, I was told, that the only reason for the union had to be for profit. Which, of course, was nobody's business. But I could honestly say that he was the most unattractive man I'd ever seen.

The role this woman was playing did not fit her. I couldn't help feeling that she was dramatizing the situation and enjoying it for all it was worth. I wondered why. In disgust, I turned away and went thoughtfully back to the kitchen. I was still preoccupied when Father came and asked me to bring the refreshments to the dining room.

I left him to do the honors and rushed off to see how Mama was. I didn't expect to find anyone in the room. Least of all the person I bumped into. I was shocked. She was evidently surprised by my sudden appearance, for she became quite agitated, mumbled something unintelligible and hurried from the room. I watched her go. She did not once look back. What possible reason could she have had for lingering behind? I was not even sure if Mama knew her at all.

My mother was lying propped up with pillows, looking dazed, her hands resting on her stomach, motionless except for the continuous movement of her fingers.

"Mama," I called softly. She looked at me but said nothing. "You want some coffee, ma'am?"

"No, I don't want anything."

"Sure?"

"Yes. I'm not hungry."

"But you didn't eat anything all day," I protested. "If you're going to get better, you'll have to eat to keep up your strength."

"That's because you keep leaving me the kind of food I don't like."

What food was she talking about now? I wondered. Was she rambling again? Besides, I never left her food. I'd either feed it to her, when she'd let me, or wait until she ate it herself. The same was true of Phyl whenever she was available to help out. Anger now mingled with my fears. We were all praying but it seemed to no avail. I looked closely at Mama and what I saw made me want to scream out my frustrations. I began to doubt that, contrary to the beliefs that had been instilled in us all our lives, there was a God who really listened. My thoughts were probably blasphemous but at this point I didn't care.

"Why're you so quiet, child?" Mama asked.

"I was jus' thinking." My voice cracked as I said it, and she reached out a shaky hand and patted me on the arm.

"Don't worry, Adelene," she said. "Nothing last forever."

Those words could be taken either way, I thought. Little did she know that instead of comforting me, her words had the opposite effect.

"I...I'm going to get some soup for you," I said and hurried out before she could protest.

While I waited for the soup to heat, my eyes strayed to the window and I made out two blurred figures standing by the gate. I brushed the tears from my eyes and as my vision cleared, I saw they were my father and Mrs. Elliston. They were engaged in a rather earnest conversation. It seemed to me that somehow she had managed to dominate the entire afternoon.

My feeling of resentment against my father, at that moment, knew no bounds. What right had he, with Mama lying so ill, to be spending so much time being chummy with that woman when his time would have been better spent with his wife? He gave her so little of his time.

I forced my attention back to the task at hand, half filled a bowl with soup and took it into Mama. Although she protested very strongly, I managed to feed her most of it, and having done that, I felt much better. I stayed with her, feeling very protective of her. I recalled how she'd always tell us never to worry too much about any problem because there was always an answer to everything although it may not seem clear to us at the time. Where did the answer lie in this particular problem?

My thoughts were rudely interrupted when my father walked into the room.

"How's she?" he asked.

"Jus' the same," I replied. I avoided looking at him.

He stood by the bed looking down at Mama. At that moment, I would have given anything to know just what was going on in his head. He reached out, touched her and called her name. There was no response.

He beckoned me out of the room. I followed obediently although I still harbored some resentment of him. He took his time telling me what he had in mind. And when he did, I wondered if the idea was his or he had been influenced by someone.

"I think I'll have to make arrangements to get your mother to the hospital after all."

He spoke hesitantly. "She's not getting any better and she'll probably have a good chance there."

I was stunned. He knew what the doctor had said, so what was the point? Heaven forbid, if she had to die, why not let it be in her own home instead of a cold, antiseptic-smelling hospital. I could only stare at him. My heart was full to overflowing with sadness.

"What time will Phyllis be home?" he wanted to know.

"I don't know, sir," I heard myself say. "She told me that she'd be going out with Alan after work."

"Well, I guess I'll just have to wait to have a talk with her."

"You can't send Mama to the hospital!" I blurted out in desperation.

He looked surprised but all he said was, "There's no other way"

At that moment, I badly needed someone to talk to about things. I thought of my eldest brother, James, and decided that as soon as my younger siblings returned home and I'd attended to their needs, I'd take advantage of Father being home and take a quick run over to his home and get his opinion on the matter.

Father looked suspiciously at me when I told him where I was going, but made no comment, just grunted an assent. I hurried off, hoping that I'd make it to and from my destination before nightfall.

James opened the door to my knock.

"Hey, hey! What's happening, Adelene?" He greeted me effusively.

"I want to talk to you," I said, unable to match his mood.

He looked closely at me and said in a more somber tone. "You don't look too happy. Is Mama worse?"

"I...I think so." I started to cry.

"Hey, come on. Don't get so upset. She'll pull through."

"Look, we're having dinner," he said gently, "and you know how fussy Anita is about that. We'll talk afterwards, okay?"

I nodded glumly and followed him back to the dining room. Anita greeted me coolly.

I apologized to her for the interruption and declined her offer to join them. It seemed like an eternity before the meal was finished, during which time I sat there feeling like an intruder, speaking only when some remark was addressed directly to me.

"So, what's the problem?" James asked finally.

I told him of Father's plan regarding Mama and what the doctor had said.

"Oh, Lord!" he shook his head. "I don't like the sound of that, but you know the old man; If that's what he wants to do, he'll do it."

"James, I think if all of us get together and ask him not to, he might jus' listen to us."

"Girl, I'm not so sure about that."

"I jus' feel it would be the wrong thing to do, that if she go there, she won't come out alive."

"Why, for heaven's sake," Anita cut in. "Haven't you stopped to think about the advantages?"

"What advantages?" I asked with some resentment.

"Professional help, for one," she replied.

I gaped at her. Was she trying to be funny? Didn't she hear what I said? I sat there, not knowing how to respond. James came to my rescue.

"How does Phyl feel about it, Adelene?" he asked quickly.

"She don't know about it yet."

"When did he say he'd take her?"

"As soon as possible, I guess."

"I can't make it over there tonight," James said. He thought it over for a while. "But I'll be there straight from school tomorrow. How's that?"

I shrugged. "Okay, I suppose."

I felt so disappointed. I could have saved myself the trip.

"Well, I can't understand what all the fuss is about," Anita said unkindly.

"We're talking about our mother, Nita," James sounded angry. "We care what happens to her even if you don't."

"Sorry, I'll just keep my mouth shut." She got up and flounced out of the room.

I looked out to find that daylight was rapidly fading. Since my talk with my brother was not at all productive, I got up to take my leave. He offered to accompany me a part of the way, and I was glad for the opportunity to talk to him alone. There were things that I thought he should know that I would not have been comfortable saying in front of his wife. Feeling self-conscious, I broached the subject as Katherine had presented it to me.

"Adelene, what are you saying?" he asked reproachfully.

"Well, you mean you never consider the possibility of such things?" I had no intention of being put off.

"Frankly, I think it's just stupid superstition," was his vehement reply. "Something that only illiterate people indulge in to justify their ignorance."

"I am neither one or the other, James, but considering all the weird things that's been happening in an' around the house lately, it's hard not to start thinking that way."

"What weird things?" He eyed me suspiciously.

I didn't spare him the details. He stopped short and spun me around.

"You serious?"

"Do you think I could make that up?" I snapped

"My God!" He was shocked. "How come nobody let me know all this before?"

"James, you mus' understand what it's like right now. Everything's upside down. Nobody's thinkin' straight. On top of that, I'm afraid to leave her alone. If you could hear her, you'd understand."

"Jesus...I'll have to think about this," he said in awed tones. "There must be some kind of explanation."

"Well, brother, if you can find it, just let me know."

He ended up going all the way and decided to go in and see Mama. When he emerged from her room, he looked scared. He spoke briefly to Father and promised to return the next day.

What the family conference might have yielded was anybody's guess, because of two terrifying incidents in quick succession that left us more mystified.

CHAPTER 7

I had just fallen asleep after restlessly tossing about when I was awakened by a loud knocking. It took me a few seconds to collect my wits. I then recognized Phyl's voice yelling for someone to unlock the door. The noise had obviously awakened everyone. Footsteps were pattering from every direction. The dogs were barking fiercely. I hurried out but Father was ahead of everyone. He pulled the door open, and Phyl stumbled into the room. Father gripped her arm and steadied her.

"Girl, what do you mean by coming home at this hour of the night and making all that racket?" Father asked gruffly.

Phyl didn't answer. She looked frightened, and she was visibly trembling.

"You'd better sit down and pull yourself together," Father said in a lighter tone as he took her arm and guided her to a chair.

I glanced at the door, which was still open. Eerie shadows cast by overhanging trees danced in the moonlight. I quickly slammed it shut and locked it. The dogs were still kicking up a fuss.

"What happened?" Father asked.

"Nothing," Phyl said in a shaky voice.

I looked at her and wondered. That kind of behavior was not at all like her. She was not easily moved by anything. She'd been that way for as long as I could remember. So whatever had spooked her had to be something out of the ordinary.

Father didn't press her for an explanation, but after watching her thoughtfully for a while, he said, "In the future, I'd appreciate it if you'd come home at a decent hour, young lady."

Phyl didn't respond. She had not yet regained her composure. I tried catching her eyes but she avoided looking at anyone. Curiosity was killing me. I drew closer to her. I was feeling very suspicious.

"What'd you see?" I asked in a whisper.

She shook her head, persistent in her denial. I didn't believe her, and I knew that I'd just have to wait until she was ready to talk.

Father shook his head in bewilderment. He told us all to get back to bed and started back toward his room. He had only taken a few steps when it happened. There was a loud scraping sound as if something huge was being dragged across the roof, followed by rending sounds at the windows.

Father stopped dead in his tracks, a shocked look on his face.

"What in God's name is that?" he wanted to know.

Nobody said anything. *Now*, I thought maliciously, *he'd understand.*

"Well?" he looked at each of us in turn. When everyone kept silent, he went and got his gun, walked purposefully to the door and yanked it open. "I'll soon find out."

He was gone a long time during which we stuck close together fearfully awaiting his return. Suddenly, a pitiful wail reached us from Mama's room. We moved simultaneously, jostling each other in our haste to get to her.

"*Ooooh, ooooh!*" she cried. "I can't stand it. Ooooh, no more, pleeease!"

I gently shook her. Phyl grabbed her wrist. Both their hands shook. I looked at my sister. Her expression was unchanged.

"What d'you think?" I asked in a whisper.

"I don't know what to think," she replied in kind. She looked slowly around the room as if she expected to find the answer there. My heart sank.

Suddenly, a loud popping sound made us all jump and instinctively huddle together.

It was most definitely a gunshot. What had our father found? He returned looking and sounding quite mad.

"Nothing out there," he said.

I wasn't surprised. But why had he fired the gun? As a warning maybe? If I was worried before, I was doubly so now.

That night was the longest I'd ever experienced. Because of all the drama sleep was impossible. There was a sense of urgency in my desire for the breaking of dawn. I had finally decided what to do, and was now more determined than ever to see it through, no matter what the consequence. It was the only alternative.

Father left for work next morning before Phyl stirred out of bed. Whether the incident of the night before had in some way affected his decision to get Mama to the hospital, I didn't know. But he had not tried to see Phyl that morning and I was very glad for the delay. I took advantage of my sister being home to run what I considered the most important errand.

I returned home feeling as if a load had been lifted from my shoulders.

That good feeling was short-lived, however, when later that afternoon, there was an indication that we were headed for more trouble.

Although my younger brothers attended the same school, it was not unusual for them to return home separately, though within short intervals. Consequently, there was no need for concern when Andy did not get home on time. He knew the rules and had always obeyed them.

It was Janet who first voiced her concern. Andy always helped her with her homework, and it made her more conscious of his absence. I told her to give him a little more time to show up. But another thirty minutes slipped by. She kept running back and forth to the window, looking out for him. I didn't let on that I was worried too. Soon it would be dark, and there was no telling what the night might bring.

Paul kept blaming himself that he hadn't waited for him after school. How could he have foreseen anything going wrong? We could not deny that all was not well. I finally decided that I had to go and find him.

"How?" Paul asked.

"Well, I'll jus' start walking and looking," I said with more confidence than I felt. "Both of you stay close to Mama. Don't let her know anything."

"But you can't do anything alone," Paul protested.

"If James comes before I'm back, tell him where I am."

"All right. You be careful," He issued the warning self- consciously.

I headed toward town. I had to pass the school. As far as I could see, the grounds were deserted. I scanned the streets, looked into shops, even a bar, ridiculous as it seemed. There was no sign of him anywhere. I started back home, hoping he would be there. James' car was parked in our gravel driveway, and he met me at the door with the question that dashed my hopes.

"You'd think he'd be more considerate knowing that Mama is so sick," James said crossly.

"I think something's happened to him," I said worriedly. "He's never done anything like this before"

"There's always a first time for everything," James reasoned.

I shook my head, unwilling to accept that he'd deliberately choose to do something out of the ordinary that he knew would aggravate the present situation. Since Mama had been ill, he'd rush in to see her the minute he got home from school, as if that was the only thing on his mind all day. I asked Paul if he knew of any friends that Andy may have visited. He didn't.

"We have to find him," I said wearily.

"I'm coming this time," Paul declared.

"No!" I spoke more sharply than I'd intended. "I'll go with James. You have to stay here. See that you lock the door and don't open it for anybody but the family."

"You always bossing people 'round," he grumbled.

"Well, Janet can't stay in the house alone with Mama so sick," I pointed out. "She's too little."

"That's the only thing that can keep me here," he gave in grudgingly

"Both of you stay in the room with Mama. It's important, you understand?"

"Yes."

"Don't stay away long, Adelene," Janet pleaded. She was frightened, and I couldn't blame her.

I promised I'd make it back as soon as possible.

We left in James' car. He drove slowly around the neighborhood, stopping every now and then to make inquiries of passersby, but no one had seen Andy. Finally, he decided to take a road that led out of town. I had my doubts but kept quiet about them.

"I suppose you know that if we don't find him, we'll have to go to the police?" James said after a long silence between us.

My heart skipped a beat. It had not even occurred to me. Why, suddenly, had our once-tranquil lives been turned upside down? And what force were we up against? Nothing seemed real. I struggled with the decision to confide in him. What I needed more than anything was someone to understand my point of view, why I thought it absolutely necessary to pursue the course I felt bound to take. I'd had enough opposition and I was not in the mood for more of the same.

"I feel so discouraged," I said.

"About what?"

"Everything."

"You must have faith," James said solemnly. "That's the only way to overcome difficulties."

"I know, and I try, but it's very hard when things keep getting worse instead of better."

"That's the whole point," he responded "It's a kind of a testing ground. You know what I mean?"

"I guess so."

I spotted a figure in the distance and leaned forward to peer into the darkness.

"Think that's him?" James asked hopefully.

"I'm not sure. Could be."

"We'll soon find out," he said.

Whoever it was seemed in a great hurry. My hopes fell when I recognized the son of one of our neighbors.

He was also a friend of my brothers. James stopped to question him, but all he could tell us was that he had last seen Andy after school heading toward home. If that was the case, why had he changed direction?

We debated our next move and James decided to continue on the same course. A short distance along that route was the beginning of a thickly wooded, hilly area stretching about a mile or more. As we approached it, memories of my childhood came flooding back. I shuddered as I thought of how gullible we all were then. I could still see the expression on Mama's face as she warned us never to linger there, and to be sure we were never alone when traveling.

We were told stories of men who practiced the "black arts" (I never fully understood what that meant) who enticed children with candies and other goodies and then take them into the woods where their young hearts would be taken out by those vicious men.

I remembered how terrified we were, how we would travel in small groups to and from school, running so fast I could feel the wind pounding in my ears. As I grew older, I began questioning those stories and concluded that they were fabricated by parents who conspired to use it for the sole purpose of keeping their children in line.

It was in this area that we found Andy stumbling along, his bag of books still slung over his shoulder. I almost panicked. His shirt was torn and bloody and there were scratches on his face. He had a wild look about him, and he appeared not to recognize us as we approached him.

"Andy, what happened to you?" I asked.

He didn't answer, but kept walking as if he were in a trance. James grabbed his arm to stop him.

"Man, look at you!" he said crossly "Were you fighting?"

There was still no answer. He did not even look at us.

"Andy!" I tried again, "You know you're not supposed to be out so late. Everybody fretting for you."

He just stood there staring into space.

"Look, we're just wasting time," James said. "Something's not right here."

We got Andy into the car. James and I gave up trying to communicate with him after a while.

Father met us outside. I could see by the look I knew so well that he'd planned to tan the hide off Andy. However, by the time we got Andy out of the car, he was so weak he had to be assisted inside. On closer examination, we discovered that he had a gash on his left forearm caked with blood that obviously needed medical attention. He was also running a temperature.

Scolding forgotten, Father worked at stopping further bleeding. I hurried to make some tea. Andy had taken only a mouthful when he fainted. James and I rushed him to the hospital.

We located Phyl and quickly told her the little that we knew. She took one look at her little brother and hurried to find a doctor. When she returned, she ushered us into a doctor's office. While we waited, she tried to get Andy to tell her how he got the cuts and bruises, but he sat there, still reluctant to speak.

"He may have to stay overnight," she said, eyeing him with deep concern. "I wish he'd say something. It would help if we knew how he got those cuts."

"I guess we'll just have to give him time," James said. "It's useless trying to push him."

"You're right," Phyl agreed. "I'll see you all later. I have my hands full at the moment."

She started off, then stopped and turned back. She stood hesitantly eyeing me with a strange look on her face before she said, "Adelene, when you get home, be very careful. Don't linger outside."

Before I could question her, she turned and hurried off. I gazed at her retreating form, wondering at her remark. Coming from Phyl, it was strange indeed.

The doctor allowed us to stay while he examined Andy. After he had cleaned and stitched the wound, he told us it was necessary to keep Andya day or two for observation. I was very worried about my brother and the possibility that his indisposition would complicate matters for me.

James and I stayed a while after Andy had settled in. The doctor had given him a sedative and he seemed to have fallen asleep. James signaled to me and we both started to leave the room. We got no farther than the door when we heard Andy's voice. I could tell that James was as excited as I was as we hurried back to our little brother's bedside.

"You see it...you see it?" Andy kept repeating drowsily.

"What?" I cautiously asked. "See what, Andy?"

"The little dog...you see it?"

"Dog?" I was totally confused. "What dog?"

"Yeees, it so pretty." His voice trailed off.

"Andy," I called, shaking him gently. "Andy!"

He did not respond.

"Hey, man, wake up!" James called anxiously but to no avail.

We stood there watching him a few minutes longer. His breathing was deep and even.

James shook his head, a puzzled frown on his face.

"We'd better leave him. Maybe tomorrow he'll be more rational," James said, then added.

"At least he talked."

"Yes," I agreed, "except that it didn't sound like he was really talking to anyone but himself."

"Hmm, you're right." The frown on James' face deepened as we left the hospital. We were halfway home before he spoke again.

"What do you really think about this thing with Andy, Adelene?"

"I think it's time we all wake up and face the truth that we are all trying so hard to hide from," I replied.

"And what's that?" he demanded.

"None of this is normal," I said evasively. I wasn't willing to say exactly what I thought.

Not then anyway. What Andy had said kept going round in my mind. Was it delirium or something far more sinister? I had the troubling thought that it was connected to something I already knew, but it kept eluding me. *God!* I groaned inwardly. *What's next?*

Everyone was anxiously waiting for news of Andy. My father, for the first time, had a different expression on his face. I hoped that he was, at last, taking a deeper, more serious look at the strange occurrences.

"So, what's the result on the boy?" he asked.

James explained everything, omitting only the few words Andy had spoken.

"Well, anyone who can't hear must feel," Father said, sounding angry.

My God! I thought. *How could he be so unsympathetic?* Masking my anger, I left them and hurried to Mama's room. In my distraught state of mind, I stood looking down at her lying there so still. She was on her back, her arms folded on her chest. In the lamp's dim glow, she did not appear to be breathing. I leaned closer but saw no sign of life. Horrified, I let out a piercing scream. Father came running with James close behind.

"What's the matter?" they asked simultaneously.

"Mama's deeead!" I wailed "She's deeeead!"

"Nonsense!" Father said. He looked frightened as he reached down and felt Mama's neck, then started to shake her. "Liz...Liz!" he kept calling. "Wake up...wake up!"

After what seemed an eternity, Mama moaned, shifted slightly, and spoke in a hoarse whisper.

"The heat, so hot, killing me." Her voice grew a little stronger." Get that animal out of here! Get it out!"

Her chest was heaving from the effort it took to speak. Her unwavering gaze fixed at a point by the foot of her bed on something she alone could see. It sent a horrible chill up my spine. I was afraid to look at her as I tried to stem my tears. It was then that the thought that had eluded me became focused and I made the connection.

"Oh, Jesus!" I said aloud, the words caught on a sob. "Oh, Jesus!"

"Pull yourself together, Adelene," Father said with unusual gentleness. "I understand how you feel, but carrying on won't help your mother."

He was right, of course, but I just couldn't help myself. I had to find release or burst.

James still hadn't found his voice. He just stood there, very pale, looking down at Mama.

Father was holding Janet very tenderly and comforting her, while Paul unashamedly kept brushing the tears from his cheeks. I impulsively grabbed James's arm and pulled him out of earshot.

"You remember what Andy said?" I asked between dry sobs.

"Andy didn't...," he began, then paused and stared at me. "You...you mean about a dog?"

"Yes, I think it's the same one Mama's seeing."

"Seeing where?" he looked blank.

"At the foot of her bed. Didn't you hear her in there?" I asked impatiently. "She's been saying it all the time."

"Stop it, Adelene. For God's sake. You're giving me the creeps."

"So how do you think I feel dealing with it every day?"

"Do you really believe she's seeing things?"

There was still an element of doubt underlying the question. I couldn't blame him. It sounded too unreal. Before I could answer, Father came out to join us. He was shaking his head the way he usually did when he was baffled. He told Paul and Janet to go to bed and not to worry.

It was at that point that I was suddenly gripped with a strong premonition that at no cost should Mama be left alone. I said a hasty goodnight to James with the promise of continuing our conversation the next day. I quickly collected my pillow and sheets from my room and settled down in a chair at my mother's bedside.

Father was sympathetic to my need and made no protest. He just went off to rest on the settee as he had been doing the past few nights.

CHAPTER 8

I kept an all-night vigil at my mother's bedside. Sleep was impossible, not only because of the lack of proper accommodation, but I was tormented by my thoughts. As the night dragged on, I prayed many silent prayers.

Some time far into the night, I must have dozed off. To this day, I cannot be sure because what I experienced then was as real to me as life itself. I remember becoming aware of a presence in the room. Thinking it was my father, I thought to look around but was alarmed to find that I could not turn my head. Neither could I get my arms and legs to function. I was being held down by an intangible force over which I had no power.

In a panic, I tried to call out for help, but no sound came. Somewhere in my subconscious was the thought that I must not succumb to the force. I had to keep on fighting; I had to overcome. I had to pray.

A voice seemed to say. "Inject something spiritual to ward off the evil force." But all that I could say was, "God! God! God!" My lips moved soundlessly, forming the words over and over until a faint ringing started in my ears and then gradually subsided and the sound of my voice became audible again. The spell was broken. It left me feeling dazed.

Gradually, the fear that had become my constant companion assailed me. I remained still, moving only my eyes to scan the room.

Close by was an unmistakably loud sniff and the soft pad of feet moving past me toward the door. Relieved that I had good company, I was about to reach out a hand when my mind cleared sufficiently to warn me that something was very wrong. None of our dogs would be inside the house at that hour. I swung around to look at the door. It was only slightly ajar.

Willing myself to get out of the chair, I turned up the light of the lamp to check on my mother. Thank God, she was still breathing. Before I could settle down again, Father came in to check on the sounds he'd heard coming from the room. He'd thought that Mama was better and we were conversing, knowing full well that he would no doubt scoff at the truth.

I told him quite simply that I must have been talking in my sleep. He gave me an odd look and suggested that I go to bed and that he would take over. I politely refused, for the simple reason, ridiculous though it may seem, I could not shake the feeling that my presence alone would make the difference between life and death. Of course, I didn't say that to him, neither would I dare say it to anyone. It was my secret. He did not press the matter. He just stood there looking down at his wife with an unfathomable expression before he left us alone again.

For the rest of the night, I kept the light at its brightest.

I was up at the crack of dawn. My body was stiff and achy from sitting up all night. But it didn't matter. All that mattered was my mother's welfare.

As soon as Father left for work and I'd seen my younger siblings off to school, I went purposely to have a talk with Phyl. Fortunately for me, it was her day off from the hospital.

As usual, she was cross at being disturbed, but for once. it didn't bother me.

"How's Mama?" she asked groggily.

"Bad, can't be worse."

That got her attention. She sat up and reached for her robe, which was hanging on the bed post.

"I've come to tell you that I have to go out, so you'll have to watch her."

"Where are you going?"

"Er...um to the shop."

She looked at me rather suspiciously. I think she knew that I was lying, but made no comment. I hurried out before anything more could be said. Halfway down the path leading to the gate, I realized that I had forgotten something very important and dashed back into the house.

Phyl.was already in the bedroom with Mama.

"Thought you'd left," she commented.

"Yes, but I forgot the money," I lied again.

I rummaged through a couple of drawers to find what I'd really returned for.

"What are you doing searching through Mama's things like that?" Phyl sounded disapproving.

"Mind your own business," I snapped.

"Why are you so nervous?" she persisted. "What are you up to, Adelene?"

"Up to nothing." I found what I was looking for and quickly balled it up in my hand.

"What you got there?"

"Nothing." I pushed the drawer in with my knee. "See you."

"Adelene!" she called after me. I pretended not to hear and rushed out. It was not easy keeping my secret, but I could not risk sharing it at this point for fear of getting any negative feedback. I was determined to pursue my course.

Katherine was already waiting for me at the crossroads as we had arranged the day before. We started off without speaking. We were moving toward, what was for me, an unknown world. As we trudged along under the rising temperature of the mid-morning sun, I was informed that we were going to a "Mission house" for a reading by a spiritual healer professionally called "Mother." I would then know what action to take. It all sounded very scary to me. But Katherine assured me that there was nothing to fear. "Mother" was a religious woman and her only aim was to do good. I had to believe Katherine or lose hope.

The wooden gate leading to the Mission was guarded by a burly man with stern features. He was wearing a red turban and an ankle-length robe of the same color. A white sash was slung across his right shoulder and was tied in a knot over his left hip. Stuck in the knot was a braided rattan switch, looped at one end to guarantee a sure grip. In his right hand, he held a shepherd's staff firmly resting on the ground.

"Wat is your mission?" he asked in a surprisingly soft voice.

Katherine explained and he stepped aside for us to pass through the gate. The Mission house was not as I had imagined. It was built more like a shed with a sloping zinc roof and wattled sides.

Inside were crude benches set in neat rows facing an altar set on a dais, draped with a white cloth.

There was no sign of anyone and as I stood uncertainly surveying the strange scene, a voice spoke out of the silence. I jumped.

"If anyone is walking with doubt or fear, turn now and return from whence you came. I want no unbelievers here."

I looked around guiltily. The words were spoken by a woman who had materialized in front of the altar. She was of slight build and dressed in white from her mountainous turban and long, flowing robe to her shoes. She was looking directly at me, and I had the uncomfortable feeling that she could read each thought as it was formed in my head. For a while, I stood somewhat undecided before I moved forward with a pounding heart, and stopped in front of her. I was very nervous and tried not to show it. Before I got up enough courage to address her, she shook me up still further when once again she spoke in a loud voice.

"Too late, too late, shall be your cry!" She closed her eyes, sucked in her breath and her entire body shook as though afflicted by the ague. She then became still, moaned a few times, and opened her eyes. She seemed in a daze. Her voice was much softer when she spoke again.

"With God, all things are possible, but you must believe."

"I believe," I heard myself say. I wanted to hold on to that. In the few minutes since we had met, I was plunged into despair and brought back to hope.

"Mother" turned around and motioned Katherine and me to follow as she walked through a concealed entrance into a small room. In the center of the room was a small, round table, which was also draped with a white cloth. On the table between two red candles was a tumbler half filled with water. In it stood a single green leaf from a plant known as "The leaf of life."

I was instructed to put a silver coin of a small denomination in the glass. I fumbled for the coin. My hand shook as I dropped it in.

"What is this person to you?" the woman asked, looking from me to Katherine and back again.

"My mother," I said.

"I'll need something that belongs to her," she said.

Katherine had warned me about this and I was prepared. I handed her the bandana that I had smuggled out. She rolled it up, placed it in front of her on the table, lit the candles, and closed her eyes. After a moment of silence, she began muttering some unintelligible words.

I looked questioningly at Katherine. She shook her head, warning me to be quiet. Added to my anxiety, I began to have doubts.

The woman was now holding the bandana tightly, her body going through a series of convulsions as she swayed from side to side.

"She's very sick," the woman said. "She's supposed to be dead in nine days."

I gave a cry and clapped my hands over my mouth.

"There is an evil spirit moving among you. It takes many forms. It moves by night and by day. But good can conquer evil. Your mother is a good woman. She is a strong woman, too, but you must act quickly or it will be too late."

I sat as if paralyzed. I couldn't think of anything to say because my thoughts were all muddled.

"There are many who call themselves friends but are wolves in sheep's clothing. They'll laugh with you, then stab you in the back. Beware of friends, beware of the gifts they bring. Not all showing of the teeth means laughter."

I realized as she spoke that I had to find my answers in her cryptic remarks. And, as I started putting things together, my fear increased until I had difficulty breathing. I thought of all the bottles of homemade brew my father had been bringing home that we had been trying to feed to Mama to build her strength as we were told. It struck me then, that none of us knew what they consisted of or who had sent them. Could this be the source, with my father an unsuspecting courier? Or a willing one? I rejected the latter. It was too horrible for contemplation.

The woman stopped speaking and was once again muttering in that unintelligible language.

She moved her hand in a circular motion three times around the glass, opened her eyes and looked fixedly at me. Katherine nudged me sharply in the side and whispered to me to say something. I pulled myself together with an effort and asked the woman what I should do.

"There is very little time," she said. "You must get your mother out of the house at once."

Everything flashed through my mind in quick succession. The strong feelings my father harbored in opposition to all spiritualists could not be ignored. And there was also my sister's skepticism to reckon with. It had not occurred to me that any action had to be taken outside our home. There was absolutely nothing I could do alone. I needed the full cooperation of at least one other adult member of the family.

"Is that the only way?" I asked. "Couldn't you come to my home instead?"

The woman shook her head.

"I don't work that way. You must bring her here to the Mission. That way we can work fast without interruption."

"How long would she have to stay, ma'am?"

"I can't say, but you're not to worry," she said patiently. "She will be safe here."

Heaven above! I thought, my heart sinking. There was no way this side of creation I would ever be able to accomplish that. It was bad enough that I had embarked on this quest, regardless of my reasons, but to move Mama from home to bring her among strangers in her present state would be taking things just a little too far. Especially since there could be no written guarantee as to her recovery. I was sufficiently convinced by the plausibility of what I had heard that it was necessary to try a new approach regarding my mother's illness, but there had to be another way. In my confusion, I turned to Katherine.

"De way Ah see it is dis. You mus' consider two tings an' decide which one is more important." she said.

"What two things?"

"A chance fa yur mama to get better or yur papa getting mad wit' you." She gave me a stern look and continued with a note of urgency. "Adelene, you wi' fine that some t'ings more important dan some, an' you have to mek a choice no matter wat it cost. You get me meaning?"

I looked from her to the woman whose eyes were again closed. She was moving her head from side to side. She started humming, intermittently making little gasping sounds that were accompanied by light tremors of the body. I stared, fascinated, not knowing what to make of it. Then she spoke, jangling my nerves even more.

"I see a boy... a young boy, yes, a lot of beds, people in white. Not serious. Will pull through. The dart is not for him."

"Andrew!" I gasped. "The hospital!"

She carried on as if I hadn't spoken. I looked at Katherine, who was regarding me with a questioning look in her eyes. In my concern for Mama, I had forgotten to tell her about Andy.

Now was not the time.

We waited for "Mother" to recover from her trance. I could not think clearly. I kept formulating and rejecting plans, but still the question remained. *How?* How could I accomplish what had to be done? I bowed my head and tried to pray. When I finally looked up it was to meet the intense gaze of "Mother."

I think it was what I read in her expression that influenced my decision. Somehow between Katherine and me, a way would be found to get the help necessary for my mother. How my father felt no longer mattered. As we prepared to leave, "Mother" issued another of her veiled warnings.

"Don't let the right hand know what the left hand is about." She gave a faint smile as she waved goodbye to us.

"What a strange woman," I remarked to Katherine when we were safely out of earshot.

"She wise, dat's wat I know," Katherine said with reverence "I could tell you tings dat Ah witness wit' me own two eyes, you would never believe."

"I believe you," I said, not fully convinced that I did.

"Good!" she said sounding pleased. "So now we can stop all de foolin' 'roun' an get down to business, right?"

"Right." I agreed.

When I returned home, I found Phyl puttering around in the kitchen. Katherine had discreetly waited outside ready to come to my aid when the time was right.

"So, you ready to tell me what's going on?" Phyl demanded. "Where'd you go with Katherine?"

"To get help for Mama," I said defiantly.

"What kind of help?"

I didn't answer. *Why was she pretending?* I tried not to show my annoyance.

"Well, I sure hope you know what you're doing." she went on.

"Yes, an' regardless of how you and Father think, I have no intention to sit here an' watch my mother waste away to death."

"She's my mother, too," Phyl said resentfully, "and I love her as much as anybody else."

"But you're too straightlaced to go outside your profession to seek help for her." I was getting angrier by the minute. "You think your doctors are miracle workers. You think they're God!"

"Okay, cool down, cool down." Phyl. said, holding her hands up as if warding off a blow. "What you plan to do?"

I was taken aback by her response. I calmed down enough to give her a quick summary of the day's events and what my plans were.

She sat silent for a while, then surprised me by saying: "Maybe it's worth a try. But how're you going to get Father to agree?"

I turned away without answering. I had things to do.

"Adelene! You don't mean to...." She broke off, too shocked to complete the question.

Her mouth agape.

"Yes." I tossed my head defiantly. "I'm going to do it right now. It will be too late for him to do anything about it by the time he's home."

"There will be hell to pay," Phyl warned.

"I know, but I don't care." I said with strong determination "My back is broad."

"I hope it's broad enough." Phyl said with a worried look. "What if something should go wrong?"

"It won't." I said emphatically. "And I'm not goin' to think that. Anyway, what could be worse than the way it is now?"

"Well, you have a point." she conceded. "I can't go with you because I have to work, but I'll back you."

I stared at her. I opened my mouth to speak, but quickly snapped it shut. Surprised as I was, this was no time to go questioning her miraculous change of heart when it had worked so well to my advantage. Memory of her dramatic entry into the house three nights ago flashed into my mind, and I became convinced that was where the answer lay.

Phyl volunteered to go and find us transportation. In the meantime, Katherine and I got Mama out of bed. In her helpless state, it was no easy task, We did not attempt to dress her, just slipped on a robe.

We experienced some difficulty getting her into the taxi. Even though she had lost a lot of weight, her body had become so rigid it was impossible to get her into a comfortable sitting position. We ended up, with the help of Phyl and the driver, with me cradling her head and shoulders on my lap, and Katherine holding her legs on hers. Through it all, the only reaction we got from our mother were a few moans.

When we reached the Mission, two attendants brought a stretcher, crudely constructed of canvas and lengths of rough wood. They took Mama to a room adjacent to the Mission, slightly larger than the one I'd been in that morning, and laid her, stretcher and all, on a small bed. Someone threw a sheet over her. Six other people came in and they formed a circle around the bed. Soon after, "Mother" entered, caught each of her disciples in turn and spun them around three times amid many hallelujahs. Then she turned and did the same thing to Katherine and me. I was scared out of my wits.

As if on cue, each person began praying his or her own prayer all at once. Their voices rose in different levels of tone, creating a confused babble of sound that seemed to have no meaning. I began to feel that I did not belong there. It was only then that I realized the enormity of my actions and the possible repercussions. Just for a moment I faltered, but I looked at Katherine and felt reassured.

Leaving Mama there to return home was the most difficult decision I have ever had to make, but I was only able to do so because Katherine offered to stay in my place—and the fact that I was needed at home.

But the worst was yet to come, and I had to face it alone.

CHAPTER 9

D uring the hours I'd been occupied with Mama,
I had not given much thought to the rest of
the family. Phyl had promised to stand by me
and I felt comfortable with the knowledge that she
would be available to explain the situation to our siblings. Unfortunately, it did not turn out that way. Phyl
had left the house and they had returned home to
nothing. I was overcome by guilt when Paul and Janet
rushed out to meet me. Janet was in tears and the fear
in Paul's eyes stabbed at my heart.

"Adelene, is Mama dead?" Janet asked between
sobs.

"Stop it, you little fool," Paul snapped. I knew it
was just to cover up his own feelings.

"No, no, she's alright." I hastened to set their
minds at ease.

"But she's not here," Janet wailed. "Where is she?"

"Yes, where is she?" Paul echoed.

"Don't worry," I said reassuringly, fervently hoping
that there really was nothing to worry about. "I took
her to a place where they take care of her kind of
sickness."

They kept plying me with questions. I had difficulty getting them to accept the fact that Mama's chances
were better away from home. The more they talked,
the less confident I felt.

It set me wondering what my fate would be if I lost my gamble. The burden of responsibility was mine alone, and may God have mercy!

That evening, to compensate for having caused them unnecessary worry, I fixed them something extra special for dinner, and was gratified to watch them, despite everything, partake of it with gusto. Through it all I was in my own private hell, uneasy at the prospect of having to face my father.

Though I tried to appear calm, I was in fact, quaking inside. I contemplated leaving the house to avoid a confrontation, but concern for my brother and little sister influenced my decision to stay. I had no wish to expose them to more unpleasantness. Besides, too much had happened the past few days and it would be grossly unfair to leave them to face any possible danger without my support.

Paul became openly hostile to me as the evening wore on, and I could only guess at what was going on in his mind.

"I wonder what Andy's doin' now?" Janet said after a very long silence.

"He's alright." I said.

"How do you know that?" Paul asked sullenly.

"Phyl told me so today,"

"I want to see him, "Janet said. "You think we could go see him tomorrow?"

"That may not be necessary," I said.

"Why not?" Paul wanted to know.

"Because Phyl thinks they'll send him home tomorrow."

"Oh, that's good."

There was such relief in his voice, it made me realize how worried he really was.

Janet stuck closely to me wherever I went in the house, to the point where it started to annoy me. Finally, I ordered her to sit down and stop making a nuisance of herself.

"I don't want to be alone when that thing come," she said plaintively.

"What thi—?" I began, but stopped and just stared at her. How could I not have understood? "Okay, come on then."

It was then that I noticed that Paul was also trailing along, but in a more subtle way, and I knew that his fear was just as real as everyone else was. I suggested that we go to my room where we could relax until it was time for them to go to bed. I needed their company as much as they needed mine. Janet talked a lot, but Paul said hardly anything until he interrupted Janet to say, "I can't bear that Mama's not here, but it will be good not to have to hear her crying out all the time."

Yes, I thought. *Those cries.* They had become unbearable, occurring at all hours of the day and night. No wonder Father had decided to take her to the hospital. My heart skipped a beat. This was going to be a long, miserable night.

Paul and Janet went out to meet Father when he arrived. I stayed in my room. But not for long. I could hear him asking for Mama. He sounded scared. Then he was calling my name, bellowing at the top of his lungs. I walked slowly out and stood a short distance away from him.

"Where is your mother?"

I kept silent, not knowing how to say what I had to say.

"Speak up, girl!" he thundered.

"She... she's not here, sir."

"Damn it, I can see that. Where is she?"

"She went out," I hedged.

"Adelene, don't play games with me. I'm sure Liz was in no condition to leave the house by herself, so you must know where she is."

"I took her to a healer," I said in a rush.

"You... did... what?"

I repeated what I'd said. I could see his mouth working but no sound came. He was so furious that I feared a heart attack.

"Who do you think you are?" he finally got out. "Who the hell do you think you are to go making decisions like that behind my back?"

"Well, Mama needed help."

"And you think that by taking her to some crazy place you'll be helping her?" He spoke with such anger.

"It can't be worse than staying here suffering, sir," I said with rising courage.

"You know, you've always been a forward child.
You think you should do as you like. But you'll pay for
this!"

I raised my head defiantly. I knew that by his
standards, I would be committing an unforgivable sin
by talking back to him, but as I faced him, I no longer
saw him as the formidable figure that he had repre-
sented throughout my childhood.

"I don't care!" I said with spirit. "You can do anything you want with me."

He looked stunned as he glared at me.

"I want you... to tell me... where my wife is right
now so that I can go and get her away from those evil,
superstitious people and take her to the hospital, and I
have no intention of putting up with any foolishness
from you. Get that?"

I could feel the force of the old influence creeping
up on me, and I moved a couple more steps away from
him.

"I'm not going to tell you, sir. I'm sorry."

"You get out of this house!" he said through
clenched teeth. "Get out! If you feel you are above obey-
ing my orders, then you are old enough to take on your
own responsibilities."

"You want her to die. That's why you don't want
me to do anything to help her," I shot back at him. I
knew I was going too far but I couldn't stop myself.

He came at me, his eyes two red balls of fire. I ran.
I was wise enough to know that if he caught me,

anything could happen. Safe behind the locked door of my room, I could hear him demanding of Paul and Janet to tell him where Mama was. When Paul reminded him that they had been in school and remained persistent in his denial that he had no knowledge of Mama's whereabouts, our father became more enraged.

"You're lying!" he thundered.

"No, sir," Paul said.

"So you all gang up against me, huh?"

I heard no response from either Paul or Janet. I was feeling terribly guilty. They were bearing the brunt for something which only I was responsible for. As I listened to my father ranting and raving, I started to weaken, but not for long. I held on to my faith in the belief that I had done the right thing by Mama. A door slammed and there was silence. I waited just a few seconds before peeking out. My brother and little sister were hurrying toward me, and they didn't look at all happy.

"See what you done?" Paul accused angrily. "What if something bad should happen to Mama?"

"Why is everyone expecting the worse?" I snapped. "Why not think that something good will happen for a change?"

"But you don't even know anything 'bout those people, You're just takin' chances."

"I know enough, and I don't want to hear anything more about it." I was very much on the defensive.

"That's because you're scared." he shot back at me. "Who you think you're fooling ?"

I thought I had done a good job hiding my emotions, but apparently not well enough to fool Paul. I was thinking of something to say when we were interrupted by a knock on the door.

We looked questioningly at each other and waited. This was no time to go opening doors. The knock came again, this time louder and more insistent.

"We'd better go and find out who it is," I whispered.

"Wait," Paul said when we were halfway to the door. "We'd better not take any chances."

He ran to the kitchen and came back armed with a large pestle.

"Now," he said brandishing his crude weapon. "I'm ready for anything."

"Who's there?" I yelled.

"Your Aunt Rose," came a muffled reply. "Open up."

"Oh." I was so relieved. I quickly unlocked the door. I had never been so happy to see anyone in my life.

"Well," she stood with her hands akimbo, pretending to be angry. Her eyes darted to each of us, then came to rest on Paul with his weapon still held high.

"You in de mood to kill somebody, boy?"

I looked at Paul and we both burst out laughing.

"Aunt Rose," Paul said lowering his arm. "You're lucky."

"Good ting, seeing Ah not ready to depart this world yet," she said dryly. "Ah come to see yur mother, Ah hear she's getting worse."

I told her as briefly as I could, what I had done. She looked at me in disbelief then started to chuckle.

"Well, bless me soul. Chile, I never know you have so much guts." She chuckled again. "It couldn't have been easy goin' 'gainst your father like that."

"I couldn't sit down an' watch Mama suffer so much," I said, pleased by her attitude. "It was terrible. I had to do something."

"You never say a truer word." She looked curiously at me. "How you come to mek a decision like that?"

"It was because of what the doctor said. And she was getting worse every day an' a good friend advise me to try that way." I did not wish to name names.

"T'ank Gawd fa that!" she said with sincerity. "That is really a good friend. Ah know nothin' would convince your father. Ah try to tell him but he wouldn't listen."

"I didn't know that, Aunt Rose," I said and wondered at what time that had taken place, also why it had never occurred to me to consult her.

"That's because nobody ever bother to take the trouble to talk to me 'bout anything important." She said it lightly but I sensed a deeper feeling. "You all t'ink Ah have a hole in me head."

"No, Aunt Rose, we don't think that," I hastened to reassure her.

"Well, so it seem to me." She shrugged her shoulders. "Ah'm used to it by now."

I felt badly for her, but I was at a loss as to what to say that would really convince her that we cared.

Janet took the opportunity to get a word in and that put an end to a moment that had become very uncomfortable for me. "Aunt Rose, you know that Andy's in the hospital?"

"What! How come?"

"He can't talk," Janet said dramatically.

"What you sayin', Chile?" she looked at me. "Adelene, what's goin' on in dis house?"

Aunt Rose looked troubled after she got the full story, which Paul and Janet were also hearing for the first time.

"Ah don't like de soun' a dis at all. Ah tink you all should take a change from dis house."

"Why, Aunt Rose?" Janet innocently asked.

"Ah tink you all in danger here, an' it's not the kind you can see."

Janet moved closer to me. Paul just sat there and stared at our aunt. Perhaps it was the way she said it that made me more afraid than ever before.

"I don't think Father would agree to that under any condition." I said quietly "We'll just have to be careful."

"You need more than that," she said thoughtfully. "Besides. Ah t'ink you should go an' stay wit' your mother."

"Any special reason why?" I asked. My throat felt dry.

"Somebody fa her should be wit her, that's all." She gave me a strange look. "Ah think you're the reason Liz is still wit' us."

"What you mean by that, Aunt Rose?" Paul cut in looking suspiciously at her, then at me.

"You wouldn't understan', boy," she said mysteriously, "so Ah wont go into it now. One day Ah'll explain."

Although we pressed her, she was adamant, saying that it was sometimes good not to know everything. Her cryptic comments set me to wondering if she could hold the answers to questions about myself that I'd for some time found quite disturbing despite my efforts to quell them. How often had I heard the unkind remark that Aunt Rose was a loony?

It struck me, as I looked closely at her, that if we had all taken the trouble to know her, we would have discovered that she was much smarter than anyone ever realized. I felt extremely good that she was on my side.

Aunt Rose had decided that she would wait to see Father to discuss the possibility of coming in to assist us. This would afford me the opportunity of giving most of my time to Mama. In the meantime, she tried to put us at ease by recounting numerous escapades from her childhood days, which kept us in stitches. I had never before seen this side of her, and it was like meeting her for the first time. I vowed then that I would create a closer relationship with her in the future.

It was growing quite late and Father had still not put in an appearance. Aunt Rose, tired of waiting, made a few uncomplimentary remarks about his behavior, which I considered totally justified. She issued a final warning for us to be very careful and started to leave when our mysterious assailant arrived.

We stood speechless through the most violent attack to date. There was an angry quality about it. This time the entire house seemed to be affected. Not only did the windows rattle as if they were being battered by hurricane-force winds, but with it came a horrible wrenching sound that made me feel that at any moment the house would collapse on us. The odd thing about it all, I felt nothing. There were no vibrations! Instinctively, we all grouped together. Janet was hugging me around the waist with all her little might.

Outside, one of the dogs yelped in agony and must have run off for his cries grew fainter and more distant. The other two were barking furiously, although this time we heard no running footsteps. Aunt Rose, looking stunned, mumbled something under her breath and solemnly crossed herself.

The racket had barely ceased when, to add to our already jangled nerves, Janet screamed and hugged me tighter, a terrified look on her face. I followed her gaze and saw the doorknob slowly turning, I dared not let on that I was close to panic. Paul, with forced bravado, armed himself in readiness to attack, The door was pushed open and Father walked in, looking around expectantly.

"Who was that I see come to the door?" he asked, totally ignoring Aunt Rose.

"When, sir?" Paul asked.

"Just before I come in?"

We all looked at each other.

"We didn't see or hear anyone, sir," I spoke up bravely. "Aunt Rose is the only person to come here, and she's been here a long time."

"That's strange. There was a tall man not far in front of me. He was wearing a white suit. so I never lost sight of him. I'm sure..." he trailed off.

"Albert," Aunt Rose spoke for the first time. She sounded angry. "You seein' what's not there an' Ah tink it's time you sit up and tek notice."

"What you talkin' 'bout, woman?" Father glared at her.

"Wat you tryin' to pretend away?" She was still angry. "There's something evil lurking 'round dis house and the sooner you own up to it and do something 'bout it, de better it will be fa yur family."

"Rubbish!" Father snapped. "I should've known you're the one behind this scheme. Well, let me tell you something, Rose, I don't want you coming here putting all that nonsense in my children's heads. You understand?"

"Nonsense, you say?" Aunt Rose scoffed, not batting an eye. "It seem to me, judging from what Ah jus' experience that de devil himself runnin' rampant 'round here."

"Well, that don't surprise me at all seeing he must've walked right in here with you."

"Say what you will," Aunt Rose retorted, "but Ah warnin' you."

Father turned away in a huff, and as I had feared, focused his attention on me.

"Girl, you ready to tell me where your mother is?"

I quailed before his penetrating gaze, but I didn't answer him. There was no point in antagonizing him further. I felt reasonably safe with everyone standing there. All eyes were now on me and I tried to think of something to say to ease the situation, but my mind was still full of what had happened earlier, and I felt a bit shaky. Aunt Rose came to my rescue.

"Albert, if you don't mind, Ah'll stay here tonight an' Ah can come in an' help in de daytime till Liz get better."

"You know she's goin' to get better?" he asked gruffly.

"Ah sure hope so."

He looked at Aunt Rose for a long time broodingly, then shrugged his shoulders and walked off, leaving me to wonder at his odd remark

"Suit yourself. Just don't get in my way," he retorted over his shoulder, and as if it had just dawned on him, he spun around and focused his attention on Paul and Janet. "Aren't you children supposed to be in bed?"

"Yes, sir."

"Then, get to it" he ordered.

Father and Aunt Rose had never gotten along. As far back as I could remember there had always been this friction between them, but I never learned the cause. Emboldened by my new rapport with her, I ventured to ask my aunt.

She stood surveying me, looking very serious, then she chuckled.

"Maybe Ah know too much," she said.

"I don't understand."

Once again, she chuckled, a deep, guttural sound that made me want to join in.

"You know, Chile, as Ah said before, sometimes it not good to know everything." She shook her head slowly, pensively. "Not good at all."

Well, I thought with keen disappointment, *so much for that, but maybe someday.*

CHAPTER 10

The next morning, I started moving about very early although I felt battered after a night of fitful sleep. I was tormented by guilt and fear. I went to the shower and let the tepid water beat down on my body. It had an invigorating effect, and I emerged feeling fit and ready for whatever the day may bring.

Aunt Rose joined me in the kitchen while I was busy putting some lunch together to take with me for my visit to Mama. It was fortunate that she had decided to stay, for with her there, it freed my mind from worrying about my younger brother and sister being alone when everything was so unpredictable, and Phyl could not be relied on due to her work schedule.

I informed my aunt at what time I expected to return and she was agreeable. I also had to be there to meet James for our planned visit to the hospital. The "Andy" mystery was still unsolved.

I left the house quietly and headed for the Mission. I half ran, half walked the two miles.

Because of my anxiety. I had eaten no breakfast but felt no hunger. Even if I had, I am sure I would not have been able to swallow even a small bite. The thought uppermost in my mind was just what would I find when I reached my destination.

I collapsed from sheer exhaustion on one of the huge boulders that stood like sentinels at either side of the gate leading to the Mission. My lungs felt as if they had expanded beyond their limit. I gulped in deep breaths of the balmy morning air, feeling as if the next would be my last.

When I was once more breathing normally, I became aware of the slow, pulsating beat of a bass drum that seemed to be keeping time to the beat of my heart. I could feel the earth vibrating as I rose unsteadily to my feet. I had the weird sensation of floating in space. It took me a couple of minutes to regain my equilibrium and I was able to move through the gate toward the small church, on top of which flew a small, white flag.

Maybe because there had been no guard at the gate, when I entered, a woman who was standing just inside the door caught me unceremoniously and spun me around three times. I saw the floor spinning up to meet me and would have fallen had she not steadied me. My stomach turned and while I battled nausea, I frantically cast my eyes around in search of Katherine. We spotted each other simultaneously and she hurried to join me.

"How's Mama?" I whispered.

"No worse." she replied in kind. "They work on her de whole night."

"What's happening now?" I still felt sick in my stomach.

"They're gettin' ready for a service, so you jus' in time." she gave me a keen look. "Don't fret so. Everything goin' to be alright."

I nodded, blinking back tears.

"Ah'm goin' to run home. Ah'll be back later, okay?"

"Okay," I managed. "Thanks."

"No problem. You tek care." And she was gone.

I was left alone in a strange world and I felt truly lost. I turned to speak with the woman who had ushered me in, but she motioned me to silence. I did not know where my mother was.

I took a seat at the back and waited.

In front of the altar, a group of twelve people, four men and eight women, stood waiting. They were all similarly clad in flowing white robes, except that the women wore red and white turbans on their heads, and red sashes, the men blue and white. The drumbeats quickened as two men came in bearing a stretcher with someone on it. I was unable to see. They set it down at the base of the altar. Immediately, the group moved to form a circle around it. They all held a green twig from a tree I could not identify. It probably had some curative or mystical power, seeing that they would raise their arms simultaneously to the beat of the drums and pass the twigs in a sweeping motion over the prone figure on the stretcher.

Suddenly the mood changed. Someone started to beat a kettle drum blending with the bass to a rising tempo, and just as suddenly, stopped. All movement

105

ceased and the woman I knew only as "Mother" walked in majestically and took her place behind the altar. She was dressed in the same manner as the day before, in full white. She raised her arms and spread them wide, her huge sleeves draped in a winglike manner. I imagined her rising in the air and flying away. With her head thrown back, she began to pray. It was a long prayer that ended in a babble of an unknown tongue.

There was more of the same among her followers, while others shouted their amens and hallelujahs. The drums started up again and the leader came down from behind the altar and joined the group. She carried a tambourine, which she was skillfully beating to the accompaniment of the drums and started to sing in a melodious contralto voice.

Oh let the power fall on me, my Lord,
Oh let the power fall on me,
Oh let the power from heaven fall on me,
Oh let the power fall on me.

This was picked up by the group as she led them with a graceful, swaying motion around the stretcher, waving their twigs as they sang the same words over and over again, getting more emotional by the minute. There was a compelling force about the whole scene and the few people who had come for the service were irresistibly drawn in.

Then, to my horror. I watched as one woman, then another, stopped singing and began making deep, guttural sounds in a chant that sounded like "*Heya, heya, heya*," their chests heaving and contracting from the strain. One woman fell in a stupor, foaming at the mouth. Another soon followed. The other dancers moved gingerly around them otherwise ignoring their plight. The song went on mingled with the chant, which was now taken up by a hoarse, masculine voice.

"Mother" was now standing by the stretcher. She was shouting at the top of her voice.

"Loose her, Lord! Loooooose her! Loooooooose her, Lord, and let her go!"

It was bedlam! I clenched my fist to try to keep my arms from shaking. Dear God!

I moaned inwardly. *What had I done?* I couldn't take my eyes away from the scene. I wanted to scream out in my misery. Instead, I managed to turn away until the silence penetrated my consciousness. Looking around, I was surprised to see the figure on the stretcher sitting up. I gasped and stared in wonder.

"Mother" raised her arms again in that angelic manner and said a short prayer of thanks. After it ended, she stood looking solemnly down at my mother. Then her lips curved into a smile that lit up her entire face. I was amazed at the transformation.

"Sister," she said. "You have been traveling on a long, dark road, but there is light ahead."

Mama seemed in a daze. Her eyes slowly roved around until she saw me. She made a feeble attempt to get off her precarious perch, but "Mother" laid a re-straining hand on her shoulder and gently pushed her back. Mama relaxed without protest, her eyes still fo-cused on me with a look of uncertainty.

Still shaky from my experience, I gave her a trem-ulous smile. I badly wanted to go to her but sensed that it would be in violation of their rules. So, I stood my ground and waited for whatever was yet to come.

Two burly male attendants came in and carried away the two women who had fallen in a trance. Mama was next. The few people who had made up the congre-gation trickled out and I was left alone, not knowing what to do. Just as I decided to go out and have some-thing to eat, a woman came up to me.

"Come," was all she said. She led me to the room where they had taken Mama. They had moved her from the stretcher to a cot. Her eyes were closed and I wondered if what I had witnessed earlier had been an illusion and that her condition remained unchanged. I looked at the woman for reassurance.

"She's alright." she said in a raspy voice. "Just talk to her, make her feel better." With that she turned and left us.

"Mama," I said, almost whispering.

My mother slowly opened her eyes and stared at me for a moment.

"Adelene, it's you." Although the words were barely audible, I detected relief in her voice. "I been lying here wondering if I was dead or alive. I feel so strange, like I'm in another world."

"That's because you've been so sick." I felt relief "You're going to get better now."

I hoped that I was right.

She fell silent again. Suddenly she gasped.

"The children! Are they alright?"

"Yes, ma'am. Everybody's fine," I assured her. She was in no condition to hear any kind of unpleasant news.

When she spoke again, whatever lingering doubts I had evaporated. I felt elated.

"I'm hungry," she said and yawned. "You have anything to eat? I feel so weak."

I wished that I'd had the foresight to bring along some porridge, which would have been the best thing, considering that she had not eaten anything worth mentioning in days.

But I could not even have imagined communicating with her, much less feeding her.

"I only have tea and some bun and cheese," I informed her regrettably.

"Give me some tea, please," she said. "My stomach won't take the other things."

I unscrewed the cap from the thermos, half filled it with tea, and very clumsily raised her head and held the cup to her lips. She sipped slowly until it was all gone. Encouraged, I was reaching for the thermos to get her some more when someone knocked on the door.

"Come in," I said.

One of the men who had taken Mama from the church came in carrying a huge wooden tub and placed it down in the only available space in the small room. No sooner than he had left, two women came in with two buckets filled with a hot, dark brew. The pungent odor created by the mixture of various herbs filled the air. I did not have to ask what it was for. Katherine had hinted at the possibility of Mama having such a bath. I laid Mama's head back on the pillow and discreetly left the room, very much concerned about her hunger.

It seemed like an eternity before the women tending my mother emerged from the room and summoned the men who between them carried out the almost-full tub.

I went in to find Mama all nicely dolled up in the pretty, pink, lacy nightgown I had brought her. Her hair was freshly combed and she looked a lot better than she had in days.

"How you feeling now, ma'am?"

"Better," she said, managing a weak smile "You have more tea?"

"Yes." But before I could get it, one of the women returned, carrying a tray on which was a steaming bowl and a spoon.

"I bring you some oatmeal. Hope you like it," she said cheerfully. "It'll help you get back your strength."

I accepted it gratefully, remembering how Mama would always tell us when we were faced with a special challenge that God would provide a solution. If I ever had the slightest doubt before, it was all clear to me now. It turned out that her meals were a part of the service.

Mama had most of the oatmeal before pushing it away and drank all the coffee that had been served with it. She was still in a befuddled state of mind. I could see the questions in her eyes that remained unasked, and I, for one, shied away from having to answer them. I could not be sure how she'd feel regarding my high-handed approach in seeking her recovery. But I felt that if I had to pay a penalty, it would be well worth it. Right then nothing could daunt my spirit. I had hope.

My mother had fallen asleep. I sat watching her and I must have looked like the proverbial Cheshire cat when I looked away and saw Katherine standing by the door. My smile widened to a grin as I tiptoed to join her.

"Ah don't have to ask," she said, matching my smile. "Miss Liz. Better?"

"Yes." I said then proceeded to fill her in on all that had happened during her absence.

She kept nodding while I prattled on. After a while, she interrupted me to ask, "You glad now dat you listen to me, eh?"

That sobered me. I tried not to think of what the alternative might have been.

"Yes, and I won't ever forget it," I said from the depth of my heart.

"Ah hope you know it not finish yet," Katherine said seriously. "Dis is a good start but plenty more lef' to do."

"Wha'...what do you mean?" I felt my elation slowly dissipating.

"You will know in time," she replied. "Nothing to fret 'bout, though."

"You sure, Katherine?"

"Sure," she said quite calmly. "Remember, you can't kill a tree 'til you dig up de root."

"Oooh, I get it," I said after I'd given her statement some thought, and I fully understood what she meant. I tried to quell the feelings of doubt that threatened the joy I felt.

Once again, Katherine offered to stay with Mama so I could go back home. Mama was still asleep. I left feeling comfortable that when she awakened, she would see a familiar face.

This time, I had no qualms about going home. After all, I had something positive to report.

I hoped that it would serve to dispel all the hostilities. To my surprise, I found no one at home, which led to the obvious conclusion that Aunt Rose had taken the children somewhere. There was this eerie feeling about the place that scared me and as if that wasn't bad enough, memories of all the ghost stories I'd ever heard flashed through my mind.

I thought of going out again, but it was already three o'clock and the sensible thing to do would be to start preparing dinner so that there would be food on the table when everyone came home. I looked around and realized there wasn't enough of anything. This meant a trip to the grocery store. A swift calculation of my resources yielded a meager amount of cash, but I figured that with careful spending, I would manage to fill the need satisfactorily.

On my way out, I thought of Phyl. She had failed to give me the support that I had needed and I could not help feeling some resentment. Preoccupied as I was with my thoughts, I was oblivious to my surroundings until a familiar voice hailed me. Looking around, I saw Mrs. Bowen standing at her gate, peering vacantly around. She looks like a lost sheep, I thought maliciously, unreasonably transferring my anger towards her. I lowered my head and hurried by. I wished I hadn't gone out.

CHAPTER 11

It was late afternoon. All around the hills and valleys were bathed in the golden glow of the setting sun. Normally I would be outside enjoying the beautiful scenery until the sun sank low behind the hills and the light of day faded into twilight. Today, it was different. There were too many things demanding my attention, and too many emotions battling inside me. I didn't know whether to laugh or cry.

I had almost finished cooking dinner when James arrived. I was glad to see him. He refused my offer of food, explaining that he had just eaten.

"So, how is Mama? I heard that you took her away," he said, sounding disapproving.

At last, I could share my good news with someone. I could see the stern look on his face slowly fade away and one of incredulity take its place.

"Girl, are you talking the truth?"

"God's truth," I said solemnly.

"Boy, I have to see for myself," he said, not fully convinced.

"You'll see." I was feeling very smug.

"I must tell you the truth, Adelene, the other night when I saw Mama I honestly didn't believe she would live till daylight."

"What's not dead, don't throw away," I quipped.

"You're right. So, if she's doing as well as you say, we'll all have to thank you for it."

"Not me," I said, unwilling to take full credit. "Katherine."

"H'm, you never see smoke without fire," he commented. He checked his watch. I put the finishing touches to the meal and left to make a few changes to my appearance.

"By the way, where's everybody?" James asked when I rejoined him.

"With Aunt Rose."

"Oh," was all he said, as if it were the most normal thing in the world.

When we got to the hospital, we found Andy sitting up in bed. He had a fresh bandage on his arm, but had not quite lost that vacant look in his eyes. He didn't react to our presence and I wondered what was going on in his head. James poked him playfully on his good arm and asked how he was.

"Not too bad," Andy said finally.

"You eating?" was James' next question.

My little brother nodded and hung his head.

"Andy?" I had to know. "What happened to you the other day?"

He looked up at me, then cast a swift look around. There was fear in his eyes.

"Nothing," he mumbled.

"Come on, man, tell us," James said encouragingly. "We can't accept that 'nothing' excuse."

Another long silence. Andy kept his head bowed, his fingers toying nervously with the end of his sheet. Finally, he looked up.

"I see this little dog."

"Where?"

"It was sitting at the gate."

"Our gate?" I asked, puzzled.

He nodded.

"How did you come to end up so far away?" James asked.

Andy cast another fearful look around, and after another long silence, during which James signaled to me not to say anything, he began his story.

He had left school that afternoon with some of his friends. They had stopped for a short time to play a game of marbles, after which he had headed straight home. When he was almost at our gate, he saw a little dog sitting on its haunches, looking quite at home. It was light brown in color, fully grown but small, and it looked clean and healthy.

Assuming that it may have strayed from a neighboring home, Andy decided to ignore it, feeling sure it would soon find its way back. He had approached it cautiously, not wanting to scare it away, and at the same time provoke an attack. However, the animal stood its ground, and Andy said he began having other thoughts. Maybe, seeing it was so tame, he would take it in and if no one claimed it, then he would keep it as his own. With that in mind, he reached for the dog.

With lightning speed, it ran off down the road, stopped, sat again on its haunches, looking at Andy as if waiting for him to follow. Which he did. The dog kept up the ruse, never giving Andy a chance to catch up to it.

"Then why didn't you stop, man?" James interrupted crossly.

"I couldn't stop."

"Wha' yu mean yu couldn't stop?" James lapsed into our native lingo, shedding his proper schoolroom speech.

Andy looked appealingly at me, then looked away. Almost under his breath, he said, "It was like something was pulling me."

James threw up his arms in exasperation.

"Give him a chance," I cut in. His story thus far didn't sound far-fetched to me. Not after what I'd gone through with our mother.

"Okay, okay," James conceded "Then what?"

The little dog had run into the dense bushes on the hillside, and he had followed, not losing sight of it. All of a sudden, it disappeared. He looked around but couldn't find it. Then he heard a rustling in the bushes ahead, and thinking it was the dog, he moved toward it.

Instead, he came upon a tall, strange-looking man standing with legs crossed, leaning against a tree, looking down at him. Andy said he had been so frightened he could not move.

He began to have strange sensations in his head, and that was all he remembered.

A brief silence ensued after Andy had finished his story. James threw me a skeptical glance before turning his attention back to our younger brother, who was once again sitting with bowed head to avoid eye contact.

"Boy," James took a deep breath and exhaled it noisily, "that is some tall story."

"It's true!" Andy said defensively.

"So what are you really saying?"

"Not sayin' nothin', James." For the first time since his ordeal, Andy showed some spirit. "I'm jus' telling you what happen."

"How did you get the cut?"

"I don't know." I saw the tears in Andy's eyes. He hung his head even lower.

"How did you get back on the road?" James kept at him.

"I don't know." This time he spoke just above a whisper.

"Oh, Jesus!" James threw up his hands again in exasperation.

"Alright, alright," I cut in quickly. "I believe you, Andy. We all know James is a Doubting Thomas, same as Father."

Andy raised his head and gave me a grateful look. At this juncture, he needed someone to believe in him. I went closer to him and patted his head to show my support. A tear spilled over, rolled down his cheek, and splattered onto the back of his hand. My heart went out to him.

James' reaction was quite different. It made him angry.

"Stop being a bloody baby," he snapped. "You're twelve years old. All you had to do was to use your head."

I gave James a scathing look, which he did not see. Andy said nothing. Listening to my big brother, I realized for the first time how much like our father he was. The same pompous know-it-all attitude. Except, maybe, where his wife was concerned. It was quite obvious to me just who wore the pants in that family. I resented his lack of understanding toward Andy.

Considering all that he had been told, James could at least show some compassion.

As I stood looking at my younger brother, I began to wonder if the dog of his experience was the same as that of our mother's. And if so, how come it had been visible to them and not the rest of us. Also, what of the man he claimed to have seen? "An evil spirit moving among you," the spiritualist had said. "It takes many forms!"

The words kept going round and round in my head. Was that the answer, then? What would anyone be doing in those woods? I shuddered and tried not to think too much on it, which was easier said than done.

"Adelene?" Andy's plaintive voice brought me out of my reverie.

"Yes?"

"Mama get any better?"

"Yes, a little, and she's going to be alright."

"Me glad," he said simply.

"Me too," I said, and that was putting it mildly.

"Father come to see me today," he went on to say.

"Yes?" I don't know why I was surprised. Despite his gruffness, he was a caring parent.

"What did he have to say?"

"He was cross, said he hope I learn my lesson."

Typical, I couldn't help thinking.

"What did you expect?" James asked. "The way you scared everyone."

"Sorry." Andy was so contrite.

"Well, what's done, is done." James' voice had softened somewhat, although he still had a frown on his face. I could only guess that he was still having trouble comprehending the strange situation in which we had suddenly and inexplicably found ourselves.

We fell silent, affording Andy only the physical benefit of our company. There was nothing more to say and nothing could be gained by harassing him with more questions when he was still so unsure of himself.

I let my thoughts drift into known and unknown channels. Savoring the past, rejecting the present and trying not to dwell too much on the future and any possible complications.

A familiar voice pulled me back to reality. I ignored it.

"Why's everyone so quiet?" Phyl wanted to know.

"Well, I guess this whole crazy business has got us all down." James drew himself up lazily from the slumped position he'd been in. "How're you, sis ?"

"Fine. Just come to check on Andy."

"How much longer they intend to keep him here?" James asked.

"He'll be discharged tomorrow," Phyl said. "Except for the wound, his physical condition is good. Time will take care of the rest"

"The rest?" James queried with raised brows.

"You know, the effects of the shock," Phyl explained. "He should get over it in time."

"That's good to know," James said.

I looked at Andy. He seemed to have brightened up a bit at the prospect of getting home. I was happy for him, not to mention the fact that his being home would make things a lot easier for everyone. I still ignored Phyl. My silence must have affected her, for she suddenly turned to me and asked:

"How's everything going, Adelene?"

"Going fine," I said sullenly. "No thanks to you."

"What do you mean by that?"

I shrugged. "If you don't know, no point telling you."

"You're being unreasonable," she bristled.

"Well, I guess it all depends on how you look at things."

"You know very well that I just couldn't stick around waiting. I have my affairs to take care of, too."

"True, but you could have been there to explain things to Paul and Janet knowing, that they probably would be afraid."

"I thought you'd have been back by then." she said defensively "Anyway, no harm was done."

"How do you know?" I challenged.

She did not answer, just stood there looking at me, then she spoke.

"Anyway, it's past. What's the point in carrying on about it?"

"Maybe you're right." I said.

"What's with you two?" James wanted to know.

"Oh, nothing." I said quickly. "Everything's okay."

He looked suspiciously at each of us in turn, then rose and aborted a stretch. I knew that Phyl. was dying to know the outcome of my trip with Mama but I purposely did not enlighten her. I didn't feel bad about my spitefulness because of the knowledge that things were going well. Under different circumstances, I would not have succumbed to such pettiness. At least, I smiled wryly, I was honest enough to admit my faults.

We left Andy looking much brighter than he had been before. James seemed anxious to get home. He left me at the gate and hurried away. I stood and watched till his car was out of sight, then ran the short distance to the house.

Before I touched it, the door swung open. Paul and Janet stood looking at me with long faces. *What now?* I wondered. I beckoned them toward the kitchen, assuming that the sounds coming from that direction were being made by Aunt Rose. It was time they all heard the good news about Mama.

After my report, I could feel as well as see the relief and joy in their faces.

"T'ank Gawd," Aunt Rose raised clasped hands and looked up." Good t'ing you was in dis house, if not..."

"Oh, I forgot..." I interrupted her. I knew what she was going to say and I didn't want to hear it. Open praise always made me feel uncomfortable. Besides, what I had done was for love of someone who meant the world to me. As far as I was concerned, I had only done my duty. "Andy's coming home tomorrow."

"Oh, goody, goody!" Janet clapped her hands and began swaying her little eight-year-old body in a graceful dance around the kitchen.

All seemed well, and I was pleased to have been able to help make them feel better.

We could not have known then that our troubles were far from over.

CHAPTER 12

By the time I made it to bed that night, I was exhausted. It took a while before my body became relaxed, and I fell asleep. I slept undisturbed through the night and was awakened at dawn by the boisterous crowing of Tom, our big Rhode Island Red rooster. It was the first complete rest I'd had in days.

I indulged in an elaborate stretch and enjoyed the comfortable pull on my muscles. I sighed contentedly. I looked across the room and noticed that the door to Phyl's room was ajar. I could see that her bed was unrumpled, which probably meant that she had stayed on for an extra shift at the hospital.

As I lay there fighting the urge to stay in bed, it occurred to me that she had been doing that a lot lately. In fact, thinking back, it had started about the time she had that scare. Was she trying to escape the night, the house, or what...?

My desire to go and see Mama overcame my reluctance to get out of bed. I had planned an early start since I wanted to return home before noon. I took a quick shower, pulled on a light, floral cotton dress and went to the kitchen to make myself a cup of tea. I was halfway through it when Aunt Rose appeared.

"H'm," she said. "You up early."

"You, too." I said, smiling.

"Ah'm not much fa de bed, Chile." She added some more water to the kettle and set it on to boil. "Ah like to get up and see de dew on de grass an' get that sweet cool mornin' air in me lungs. No better medicine than dat, Ah can tell you."

"That's true, Aunt Rose." I agreed, feeling at that moment even closer to her.

She made coffee, filled a large mug, and sat on a stool opposite me. We had talked the night before, so she already knew my plans for the day.

"Tell Liz I'll come to see her soon," she said between sips of coffee. "An' I'll stay till the children gone to school, then I'll go home an' tend to me animals an' me garden. After dat, I'll come back here, okay?"

"Okay, Aunt Rose, thanks a lot."

"No need." She waved a hand impatiently. "Ah care 'bout me dear sister an' her children, dat's all."

I finished my tea, fetched the bag that I had already packed with fresh clothes for my mother and left the house. I walked at a leisurely pace and tried not to focus my thoughts too much on Mama's condition. A catchy little tune I'd learned at school popped into my head and I started humming and whistling it over and over. I guess my preoccupation with it had dulled my senses, for only when it was too late did I become aware of a familiar sound that sent my heart leaping to my throat. I quickly looked around for a place to hide, but it was too late.

"Well," my father said as he reined in his horse in front of me. "You're going to take me to your mother now, huh?"

I stood sullenly, unable to look up at him. I made an attempt to turn back, but he quickly blocked my way. I couldn't outrun a horse! It was embarrassing being caught like that and it aroused my ire. With a defiant toss of my head, I resumed my journey at an even slower pace than before. The horse's hooves clop-clopping behind me on the unpaved road.

Today, the guard was at the gate, looking sterner than ever. He nodded curtly in response to my greeting, and turned his attention to my father, who was dismounting from his horse. He informed him that the animal would not be allowed on the compound. Father made no attempt to disguise his annoyance. He muttered something unintelligible while he looked around for a suitable place to tether his horse.

I took the opportunity to hurry through the gate, which was opened just enough to allow in one person at a time. Katherine had promised to be with Mama and above all else, I could not risk having my father even suspect that she was involved in any way.

I was fortunate in immediately locating Katherine. She agreed that it was wise to keep a low profile. She had just made it through a back door when I looked around just in time to see Father enter the Mission. He came and stood beside me.

"So," he demanded, "where is she?"

"I...I don't know, sir." It was a lie, but I felt I had to stall him, all the while praying he would not try to mess things up.

"Adelene," he said in a controlled voice. "Don't provoke me."

"I have to wait until they come for me, sir."

"Till who come for you?" He was beginning to get angry.

"Somebody here. I can't just walk in."

"You'd better..." he stopped short, I sneaked a glance at him, then followed his gaze. I had not heard "Mother" come in, but there she was standing a few feet from us. She was staring at my father with open hostility. I didn't know what to make of it.

"Is this man connected to you, Miss?" she asked.

"My father." I informed her.

"Oh, yes." She drew in a deep breath. "The great man whose wild ways bring sorrow."

I glanced quickly at my father. The implication of those words was too great to ignore. The look on his face made me look quickly away. I was embarrassed for him, for there was definitely no friendliness in "Mother"'s tone.

"I have come here to take my wife home," Father said gruffly. "If you're the one responsible for keeping her, jus' tell me where to find her and I'll get out of your way. And if you give me any trouble, lady, I'll get the police."

If he had intended to intimidate her, he had miscalculated. She remained calm and only a quick lift of her head revealed her defiance. Without turning, she said, "Go to your mother, young lady. She's waiting for you in the same room."

Relieved, I thanked her and walked away.

"Wait a minute, here. What about me?" Father's voice was raised angrily.

"I'm sorry sir, but I can't let you in there." Her voice was still calm. "Unfortunately, as things stand, you are more foe than friend right now."

"What you talkin' about, woman?" Father demanded. "It's my wife I want to see."

I slipped behind the connecting door and stood there, my heart pounding, feeling shame for my father. He was a proud man, used to giving orders and having them obeyed. To find himself in such a situation would not sit very well with him. But he was facing a fearless foe, and I knew instinctively that he could not win. I stood rooted to the spot. That last remark of 'Mother's' had me wondering if after all my father was the key to the mystery we were trying so hard to solve.

"Sorry, sir," "Mother" was saying. "You'll see your wife soon enough. Right now is not the time, so I'm asking you nicely to leave because I don't want any trouble."

"That's exactly what you going to get if you keep up this nonsense."

"You're wasting your time threatening me." She had not even raised her voice. I marveled at her control. "Nothing you say will frighten me, so just be a nice fellow and go in peace. You can come again in a few days, then we'll see."

I didn't wait to hear more. Listening to my father being humiliated brought me no satisfaction, but the altercation had left me with much food for thought. It had triggered once again the suspicions that I fought so hard to lay at rest because I was so afraid for them to be true.

Mama greeted me with a faint smile. She was sitting in a chair by the only window of the room. It overlooked a fenced backyard that accommodated at one end a small chicken coop, and at the other, a vegetable and herb garden. She looked a lot better and I rejoiced in the fact. She still did not seem inclined to talk too much, but she listened attentively while I babbled on about the things I thought she would like to hear. I omitted telling her that Father had tried to see her and was perhaps even still on the compound.

I was puzzled by the fact that she had not once mentioned him. It was not normal. Was I building my hope of a complete recovery too high? What if the ordeal had affected her mind somewhat? What then? I fell silent on the thought and brooded.

"Now, what you worryin' about now?" Her voice, perfectly normal, startled me.

"You," I confessed. "I wasn't sure if you... you... " I trailed off, not knowing if it was wise to say exactly what I had in mind.

"If I'm going to be quite well again?"

Once again, she had accurately guessed my thoughts. It was uncanny. I nodded in response but kept my eyes averted so she would not see how tear-filled they had become.

I blinked rapidly but was unable to keep the tears from spilling over. I was mad at myself for being so weak, but I could not help the way I felt about this woman, my mother, who had dedicated her life to the care and upbringing of her family.

Mama patted me on the shoulder and assured me that she was fine, that everything was going to be all right. I pulled myself together after much sniffling and blowing, then to hide my embarrassment, I giggled mirthlessly.

"Come now," Mama said gently but firmly. "I don't want you to keep on fretting about me. No sense in wearing yourself out that way. You're too young for that. Jus' have faith, eh?"

"Yes, ma'am." I felt humbled.

"As I understand it, if it wasn't for you, I probably wouldn't be talking to you now. The Lord alone knows where you got the courage, but I'll always be grateful to you, my child."

I said nothing in response. I didn't want her to ever feel obligated to me. That's not what this was all about. It was about caring and loving feelings that were not restricted to family alone. I, in all honesty, could not take full credit for her survival, and it was time she knew the truth. Mama expressed no surprise when I acquainted her with the facts to date. She only smiled and repeated that it took a lot of courage on my part. I realized then that she had deliberately avoided any mention of my father, although there was no doubt in my mind that in reference to my courage, she must have been thinking of him.

The most puzzling thing of all, although she had not quite recovered from whatever it was that had affected her, she had expressed no desire to return home. Why was she so content to stay at the Mission? What was she not telling?

"You must know, Adelene, that I have a lot on my mind," Mama said slowly, deep in thought. "I have to work out how I must conduct my life from now on."

"What do you mean, Mama?"

"We won't talk about it now," she spoke hesitantly. "But there will be changes we'll have to make and..." she paused but instead of following through on her trend of thought, asked about Aunt Rose instead.

"Did you say she's coming to see me?"

"Yes, ma'am."

"Good." I was disappointed but I'd just have to wait until she was ready to reveal her plans. Just then there came a loud knock on the door before it was pushed further open and a woman whom I had not seen before entered, carrying a tray with Mama's breakfast. She had a pleasing countenance but surprised me when she spoke in a raspy tone of voice, even more pronounced than all the others whom I'd already encountered. It was easy to assume that she belonged to the group of "Trumpers."

How sad, I thought. It was difficult for me to understand the dedication to a practice that demanded such physical stress. The damage to their vocal cords was no doubt irreversible, yet they continued without a thought for themselves.

She said her name was Naomi. She had sparkling eyes and a beaming smile.

"How're you feeling today?" she asked, her voice just a whisper.

"Much better, thank you." Mama returned her smile.

"Good...good. Now you jus' eat up. We havin' service at eleven o'clock sharp so you have 'nough time to get ready."

Mama took the tray and thanked her. After she left, Mama looked at the meal and wrinkled her nose. It consisted of two boiled eggs, a couple of slices of buttered hard-dough bread, and a steaming mug of creamy coffee. I was afraid she was going to refuse it, but after a brief hesitation, she ate it all up. I couldn't help feeling smug. I realized then that there was no longer any need to worry. That feeling grew to a conviction when later she walked unaided into the little chapel. The place was full. A greater number of "Mother's" followers, mostly women, were all dressed in their religious robes of white, with red, blue, and purple adornments. I had learned from Katherine that the colors were of special significance, but I did not yet know what they were.

The service that day was more emotionally charged than ever before. All around us people were being possessed by the spirit, swaying and clapping, stomping and shouting, some were falling and writhing on the floor, while others danced around "trumping" to the wild beat of the drums, which were backed by fifes and tambourines. Almost in a panic, I looked at Mama, who was standing beside me, and saw that she, too, was caught up in the moment. I felt full inside and started to tremble.

The noise was deafening. When it finally ceased, I was weak in every limb and had to sit down. I felt scared, too. What if I became like them? What kind of future would I have to look forward to? I felt a little ashamed at the thought. Whatever they were, I had seen what they had done for my mother, and for that, I would be eternally grateful. That, of course, did not mean I owed them my undying loyalty. I decided then and there not to attend any more of their services.

When it was all over, Mama was surrounded by a group of the mission workers who were all congratulating her on her recovery. The light was back in her eyes, and the smile on her face had completely erased the sad look that she had been wearing the past days. It was a joy to see.

Once we were back in her room, she became preoccupied. I tried to start a conversation but she was not paying much attention, so I gave up. It was obvious that she had something on her mind. It may or may not be anything that she wished to share with me. All I could do was wait. I tried to channel my thoughts elsewhere, without success. Just as I was becoming piqued, she spoke.

"Adelene."

I looked at her. She looked sheepish. "There's something I can't get out my mind. I don't know if it was a dream or not. I'm just not sure."

"What you want to know, ma'am?"

"When I was sick in the house, did anyone come to visit me?"

"Only the prayer group from the church. You don't remember that? "

She knitted her brows and shook her head.

"There's this picture in my mind that there was a woman poking 'round in my room."

"I don't think...Oh!" How could I have forgotten an incident that had filled me with such resentment.

"Well...," Mama said impatiently. "You goin' to tell me or what?"

With some trepidation, I told her how I'd bumped into Mrs. Elliston that day after everyone else had left the room, and how confused she'd been when she saw me. Mama drew in a deep breath and pursed her lips very tightly. Then, as if she had made a resolution, the tension left her and her face became inscrutable. The silence dragged on. When I could no longer bear it, I ventured to ask, "Something wrong ma'am?"

"My child, everything's wrong." She fell silent again, I could see that something was troubling her. I waited, hoping that maybe she might deem it fit to divulge what it was.

"I must ask you this, Adelene..." She paused, still looking embarrassed. "You happen to see anything strange anywhere in my room?"

"Like what, ma'am?"

"I can't say exactly." She knitted her brows. "It could be anything, by the bed or the bureau. It's just a nagging feeling I have. Maybe you could check and see. Just anything that shouldn't be there, I think."

I didn't know how to tell her that I never stayed long enough in her room to notice anything out of the ordinary, only the time it took to get changes of clothes for her. The truth was, the room scared me. I was uneasy at the prospect of searching for unknown objects.

"On second thought, I'll ask Rose to do it. She will have a better understanding," Mama said, much to my relief. "No sense exposing you to that kind of unpleasantness."

By mid-afternoon, at Mama's insistence, I left for home. The time I'd spent with her that day had worked wonders for me. I felt freed at last from feelings of guilt and uncertainty by which I had been so burdened. I had taken a dangerous chance, but it had paid off. Soon Mama would be back home and everything would return to normal.

As I approached the house, I could hear voices babbling excitedly. It was a welcome change from the somber mood that had enveloped everyone since Mama's illness. I wondered what it was all about and hastened my steps. Andy was home! Paul, Janet, and Phyl were all grouped around him. No one had seen me come in. I stood and watched a while before noisily clearing my throat. They all started simultaneously, a scared look on their faces.

"Wat yu do dat fa?" Paul snapped in patois. He glared angrily at me. The reaction was the same all around. I couldn't take offense because I understood. Everyone's nerves had been on edge since the advent of our spectral tormentor whose antics had not ceased to any great extent.

I was sorry for my thoughtlessness and said so. Just then, Aunt Rose came in from the kitchen.

She gave me a piercing look.

"So, wat's the news today?"

Everyone waited expectantly.

"The best in the world," I said, grinning,

They listened with rapt attention while I related the day's progress. It was gratifying to see the expressions of relief and hope on their faces.

"There must be something in all that stuff after all," Phyl said pensively. She mulled it over for a while then asked, "When are you going back, Adelene?"

"The day after tomorrow." Mama had stressed the importance of seeing Aunt Rose the next day.

"I'll go with you," Phyl said.

"How come? Don't you have to work?"

"Yes, but I'm allotted sick days, you know."

"True." I couldn't help the sarcasm. She cut me with her eyes.

By this time, all the others were demanding to know whether they, too, could go. I tried to think up as many excuses as I could to discourage them. but they were not willing to accept anything that I said. Once again, Aunt Rose came to my rescue.

"Now...now. Listen to your sister. It not good to rush t'ings."

They lapsed into silence, not at all pleased by the rebuke yet knowing there was nothing they could do about it. I felt for them but the experiences that I had had of the method used to restore Mama was so frightening that I would not willingly have exposed them to it. They would probably be scared out of their wits.

Aunt Rose announced that since it seemed clear we would all be together, she would take the opportunity to go home and attend to her affairs.

To my surprise, Phyl offered to help me with dinner. I knew how much she hated to cook, so I thought maybe this was her way of atoning for her lack of support. I soon sensed that she had something on her mind, but I had no intention of asking her anything. If she wanted to confide in me, I was sure she would do so when it suited her.

While I cut up some fresh mutton for currying, Phyl sliced onions and gathered other seasonings. We talked briefly of Andy's condition, which she said would be alright with time.

"That boy had a bad fright, whatever it was," she ended.

"It was a dog," I blurted out.

The knife she had been using fell and clattered on the floor. She bent to retrieve it then stood looking at me with wide-open eyes.

"What did you say?"

"A little dog enticed him away."

"Oh, my God!" She was still staring at me.

"What?"

She looked so upset. I waited for an answer that was long in coming. Finally, she said, "Adelene, I'm going to tell you something, but I don't want you to mention it to anyone else, okay?"

"Okay."

She gave a quick look around and came close.

"Do you remember the night Father let me in the house and he was so cross?"

I nodded. Here at last, I thought as I held my breath in anticipation.

"Up to this day, I have a hard time believing that I saw what I saw."

"What, what?" I urged.

She cast another look around and in a low voice told me what I'd longed to hear. The evening in question, she had returned home accompanied by her fiance. Usually, they would sit together on the porch and talk, but because he had some pressing business to attend to, he had left almost immediately. Knowing how warm the house could be after absorbing the day's heat, she had decided to stay out alone anyway, until it had cooled down.

Lulled by the cool breeze, she soon became totally relaxed and was beginning to get drowsy when she made out a shadowy figure approaching the house. At that point, she could not tell whether it was male or female. She became alert and wondered who could be calling at that hour. She remembered thinking it strange that she did not hear the gate, which always squeaked loudly when opened. And why hadn't the dogs barked? But then, she figured that they may have strayed to some distant part of the property, which was not unusual. Everyone from miles around knew that

Father kept watchdogs and it was customary for visitors to first call for admittance to our property.

Whoever it was, Phyl remembered thinking, was taking a great risk. Under the circumstances, she considered the wisdom of getting in the house and wait, but her curiosity got the better of her. It had to be someone with whom we were acquainted.

The caller was now close enough for her to see that it was a man dressed in a light-colored suit. He seemed unusually tall. She could not recall anyone she knew with such height and experienced a twinge of fear. She decided then that it would be safer to go inside and had started to rise when the stranger changed course and instead of heading for the porch, had turned toward the side of the house and stopped a short distance from the corner of the porch.

She could then see him clearly as he stood with his back toward her looking straight ahead. She then noticed that he did not seem as tall as she had first thought, and blaming her faulty vision on poor lighting, watched to see what his next move would be, while she quietly sidled toward the door. She kept her eyes glued to the intruder, who, to her dismay was gradually getting shorter until she could barely make out the form. Before her horrified gaze, it disappeared, and in its place appeared a huge dog that vigorously shook itself, sniffed loudly, and moved on to the back of the house.

By that time, Phyl explained, she had been overcome by a strange, numbing sensation that had rendered her incapable of coherent thought. She felt as if she were floating around somewhere outside herself. She remembered trying to scream but was unable to utter a sound. Her jaws felt as if they were locked together. She had no idea how long it lasted before she became overwhelmed with fear and she was able to pound on the door. She shivered, remembering.

I was so spooked by her story that I was at a loss for words. There was no reason to doubt her. Had I not also gone through a similar experience? And who would ever forget what had happened following her wild entry into the house that particular night when that tortured cry from Mama had us all running to her aid.

"I know," Phyl shrugged, mistaking my silence. "It's hard to believe. That's why I kept my mouth shut."

"Girl, you're wrong. I believe every word you say." And I did.

I left her abruptly and hurried through the house, checking all the doors and windows.

Not that it would make the least bit of difference if we were, in fact, dealing with the supernatural. The feeling of being watched was still strong with me as I returned to the kitchen and the task of preparing dinner. Everything had stopped while Phyl unraveled her story. It was getting late. I placed a large frying pan on the stove poured in some oil and, while waiting for it to heat up, I asked Phyl why she had chosen that time to tell me about her experience.

"So you'd understand," she said, as she stood with her arms folded across her chest, watching me. "The day you took Mama to that place, I was feeling very industrious. I wanted to do as much as I could to help you out, but I had to get out of the house."

"Why?" I shot at her although I felt that I already knew.

"Girl...," she lowered her voice. "There were all kinds of sounds like footsteps, things falling and breaking and..." she drew closer to me and lowered her voice even more. "It happened so fast, but I'd swear I saw a woman walk out of Mama's room."

"A woman!" I gasped. "You sure?" Nobody said they had seen a woman before.

"Tell you the truth, Adelene, I keep wondering if maybe it was just my imagination because by that time, I was so scared, me being alone and all."

"I don't think so," I said pensively, "but I jus' can't figure it out."

"What?"

"You, Mama, Andy, and maybe even Father, all see things. How come I can't see anything, although I sense them?"

"Well, I don't know if it's true what they say, but Mama told me that I was born with a caul covering my face."

"So?' I had no idea what she was talking about.

"So, they say anyone born like that is able to see spirits.'

"Andy born with it too?'

"I don't know."

"What about me?"

"Adelene, I don't know. Ask Mama."

"Boy, I'd like to know what it's like seeing a ghost."

"Count your blessings, girl," Phyl looked at me as if I were crazy. "It's a weird experience."

I had no doubt it was.

CHAPTER 13

While we were cleaning up after dinner, Aunt Rose returned. This surprised me for I was under the impression when she had left earlier that she had intended to stay at home that night. I said as much.

"Yes," she admitted. "Ah did mean to stay but Ah got a strong feeling dat Ah should come back. So Ah let de spirit guide me."

"Oh!" I glanced at Phyl. She made a face which clearly expressed her skepticism. I looked quickly away and hoped that Aunt Rose hadn't witnessed the exchange. Phyl left us soon after, to get some rest, she said. The minute she was out of sight, Aunt Rose turned to me.

"You know, Adelene. Your sister t'ink Ah both deaf and bline," she said without rancor.

"Why you say that, Aunt Rose?" As I thought, she had seen the look.

"She's one dat t'ink Ah not right in me head." she chuckled.

"I don't think so, ma'am." Why was I defending my sister, I wondered. It was true.

"No matter," Aunt Rose said cheerfully. "When you know de truth, it set you free, right?"

"Right," I agreed.

144

She did not dwell on the subject. Instead, she started talking about Mama. She was very pleased at the progress Mama had made and full of praise for the healers and once more praised my timely intervention. This annoyed me somewhat. I had only done what I thought was necessary. Hoping that she could shed some light on the matter, I asked her if she had any idea how long Mama would have to remain at the Mission.

"Shouldn't be long now. Maybe another couple days. When Ah see her tomorrow, Ah'll be better able to tell."

"You sure, Aunt Rose?" the question came from Andy, who had ambled in and caught the last part of our conversation.

"More or less, sonny," she patted his head gently. "You not to worry."

At that, Andy perked up. Since his traumatic experience, there had been a noticeable change in him. He became introverted. The only thing he seemed genuinely interested in was to know when our mother would be home. I felt sorry for the little chap, and made a mental note to be extra kind and patient with him. I prayed the damage would not be permanent and that he would soon return to his former self.

With the revival of our spirits, we stayed up and celebrated with a sing-a-along. It used to be our favorite pastime, but it was a long time since we had come together in that manner.

James stopped by while we were at it and added his rich baritone to the songs we all knew and loved so well. It was great fun, and at the end, we applauded ourselves.

Long after James had left, buoyed by all the good news we imparted, we were still sitting around swapping "Anancy" stories. Aunt Rose added one I had never heard before, showing up even more the extreme cunning of that famous arachnid.

Father had not yet come in and I hoped that I'd make it to bed before he did. The embarrassing scene at the Mission was still fresh in my mind. Janet was yawning and fighting to keep her eyes open. She lost the fight and we decided to call it a night. Everyone's morale had received a boost and it was good to see Paul really smiling.

Despite my newly found peace of mind, I could not fall asleep. My thoughts were full of Phyl's story. Although I had assured her that I believed her, deep down I wondered if possibly it could only have been an optical illusion. Of all we'd been through, I think it scared me the most. It sounded so unreal. But wait! What about Andy? Had he experienced the same thing in the reverse, and had somehow missed the transformation? But he had said a small dog.

Phyl's was a large one. Father had seen a tall man heading toward the house who had mysteriously disappeared. And Mama? 'An evil spirit moving among

146

you. It takes many forms... "Mother" Robinson's words. It could not just be a coincidence. Lord Almighty! Would we ever be free? Would it be safe for Mama to come home? With great effort, I tried to put those troubling thoughts from my mind.

When I finally managed to get my thoughts centered on more pleasant things, I fell asleep to be awakened almost instantly by the barking of the dogs. They were making quite a fuss. Although I was annoyed at being denied my much-needed sleep, I knew that something unusual must have disturbed them.

I got up, went to the window and cautiously peeked out. It was too dark for me to see anything, so I returned to bed hoping that whatever the problem was, they would take care of it soon. Which they did , but so suddenly and completely that I thought it strange. I didn't dwell on it. I closed my eyes instead and tried once again to fall asleep, but became instantly alert when I detected a strange odor. I sniffed.

Something was burning, but what, and where? I quickly grabbed my robe and while I pulled it on, headed for the kitchen. The odor was getting stronger. I heard Paul yelling and I made a quick detour to his room. He was standing by the window overlooking the back yard. I saw the red glow even before I reached his side.

"Oh, God!" I gasped. "Come, Paul, we have to do something." I ran out with Paul close behind me, yelling loud enough to wake the dead, and collided with Aunt Rose.

"Wat's de matter?" Then she, too, began sniffing.

"The storeroom's on fire," I shouted.

"Wha...?" I never knew she was capable of moving as fast as she did. By this time, everyone else was awake. Footsteps could be heard hurrying from all directions. I got two buckets from the kitchen and handed one to Paul. Aunt Rose grabbed another, and with no thought of danger, in the urgency of the moment, we hurried out. We filled the buckets from the rain barrels by the side of the house and worked as fast as we could to douse the fire.

Fortunately, it had been spotted early and it was a windless night. We were still sloshing on water after we'd killed the blaze to make sure it was all out, when Father arrived.

"What in God's name happened here?" His voice was like thunder.

Everyone kept silent. I, for one, was full of resentment. Where had he been? Why wasn't he here to protect us?

"What happened?" he bellowed again.

"Well, as you can see, dis place was on fire," Aunt Rose answered for us. "We jus' manage to put it out."

"Anyone know how it happen?" I trembled at the anger in his voice. Of course no one knew.

"This fire didn't start by itself, and a ghost didn't do it either." He looked pointedly at me. I kept my mouth shut. What could I say? He was right. Someone had deliberately set the fire. One thing was clear. Whoever did it knew the purpose of the building, knew also that after the recent harvest it would undoubtedly be full and by destroying it, would be hitting us in a vital way. But who would want to hurt us in such a cruel fashion, and why?

"Paul, go get some light," Father's voice cut into my thoughts. "And hurry!"

I realized that we were all standing like zombies too shaken to even discuss the fire.

Even Aunt Rose seemed to have lost her spunk. Later, I was to discover that she was seething with anger.

While we waited for Paul's return, Father asked the question that was lingering at the back of my mind.

"What I don't understand is where's those dogs?" He started whistling for them. There was no response. I felt my heart leap as I recalled the strange feeling I had earlier.

"I think something's happened to them," I said more to myself than to anyone else.

"Why?" he shot at me.

I quickly explained.

"H'm, we better take a look 'round as soon as I check out this place."

The storeroom was small, approximately thirteen by nine feet. It was constructed of hardwood planks and had a sloping zinc roof. It was raised on concrete columns high enough for small children to move fairly comfortably under it. When we were little, Phyl and I had lots of fun playing school and shop. It seemed like a hundred years ago. We had grown up with such different personalities, separated by our individual outlooks on life.

Paul returned with two lanterns. Father took one and we all moved as one for a closer look. The lower half of one side of the structure was partially burned. Two large burlap bags, each containing several bushels of corn, were badly scorched The wood where they were resting had burned through. Father and Paul went in to assess the extent of the damage while the rest of us waited anxiously.

The dogs had still not appeared. My uneasiness grew. I kept whistling and calling their names at intervals. Nothing happened. I tried not to dwell on the possibilities. Aunt Rose must have sensed how worried I was for she suggested that we try to find them. Phyl objected, saying it was best to wait until Father could join us since no one knew what might still be lurking around, and we were defenseless. Although I knew that she was right, and despite my own fears, I was willing to take the chance with Aunt Rose backing me. However, I was saved from making a decision as Father and Paul rejoined us.

It turned out, fortunately for us, that the damage was not as bad as we had feared. Apart from the scorched bags, only a sprinkle of water had penetrated. Father said he felt that some of the produce could probably still be saved, if not for marketing, then as feed for our domestic animals. The good thing was that he did not expect a great financial loss.

Father suggested that Andy and Janet go back inside the house. Janet grabbed one of Aunt Rose's arms and pressed close to her, begging to stay. Andy gave a quick haunted look around but said nothing. I understood, but would my father? Surprisingly, he did not argue, he just shrugged and said, "All right, come on. Everybody keep close together."

We first searched the backyard, then moved cautiously towards the front. We were just turning around a corner of the house when we saw the first one. It was Floss, the only female. She was lying on her side, her legs stretched out. Something was hanging from her mouth.

Father pulled at it, but it held. Closer examination revealed that it was caught on one of her fangs, and he carefully worked it off. It was a cork about an inch and a half long, the type used to plug wine bottles. A piece of cord was strung lengthwise through it with a knot to secure its hold. Whatever lure had been attached to it Floss must have ingested it. Father muttered the one word none of us wanted to hear.

"Poison!"

We all stood in shock. Phyl asked if Floss was dead. I was afraid to know.

"She's still breathing," Father replied. "Lucky for her she didn't swallow this." He held up the object. He shook his head sadly and added, "But I don't know if we can do anything for her." *Ominous words*, I thought.

"Rose, you and the others stay here with her. Adelene, come with me."

Me!? Why not Paul? I was surprised, but despite the gloom in my heart, I felt a spark of gladness that he'd wanted me with him. Holding the lantern high, we began the search, moving slowly along the path. We found the other two dogs lying side by side a few yards from the gate at an angle where they would not have been immediately visible to anyone coming through.

I could tell the moment my father stood up after checking them that my worst fears were confirmed. They were both dead.

"My God!" Father exclaimed. I could feel his anger. "What evil beast would do something like this?"

"Oh, what a sin," I moaned. "What a sin!"

My rage and sorrow intermingled and I lost control. This was just too much after the past days of stress. My entire body began to tremble, and my heart felt full to bursting. For release, I started to whimper moving from one leg to the other. Father grabbed my arm and shook me.

"Pull yourself together, girl. Come on, calm down. I know it's hurtful, but we have to be strong."

With great difficulty, I made the effort while the tears streamed down my cheeks. I meekly followed him to rejoin the others.

"Ah tek it the others didn't make it, eh?" Aunt Rose broke her silence. All eyes turned toward me. I could only shake my head. Aunt Rose pursed her lips. I could see the restraint she was putting on her tongue, and I suspected that it was just a matter of time before she unleashed her feelings.

While we were away, someone had covered Floss with a burlap bag.

"How's this one, is she...?" Father let the question hang.

"She's still alive." Phyl answered. "We could try and save her, but I don't know if it's wise to move her."

"We have to. We can't work on her here." Father said. He stooped, put the bag more securely around Floss and very gently picked her up. "Someone hurry and get some old clothes, blankets, anything."

I hurried inside. I knew exactly where everything was kept and had them ready by the time the little procession arrived. Father instructed me to make a bed in the passageway leading to the kitchen and he laid Floss on it.

"Now look, this isn't going to be pleasant and there's nothing you children can do, so go back to bed. You have school tomorrow, right?"

"No, sir," they said hopefully. "It's Saturday."

"H'm," he grunted, not admitting to his mistake. "Go anyway."

They knew better than to argue. I took the opportunity to go with them. Maybe I was being a coward, but if Floss were to die, I couldn't bear to witness it. Back in my room, I could distinguish their voices but not what was being said. Aunt Rose probably making suggestions and Father grunting replies. In between, I heard Phyl's softer tone. I prayed. I had confidence in my father. Over the years, I'd seen him treat various diseases in our farm animals with great success. He had acquired his skill during the time he lived abroad. (I was told this was before he and my mother were married.) He rarely lost a patient, but none had been poisoned before.

This thought gave rise to a more frightening one. Whoever our enemy was, he or she proved to be quite diabolical. What would prevent the same thing from happening to our water supply or our crops? Why were we a target? What was the motive? Nothing seemed to add up. Not Mama. Not Andy. Not Phyl and worst of all, not tonight. How long would we have to endure these persecutions?

Phyl came up looking tired. She had been denied her much-needed rest, but she answered my silent question.

"Floss is still holding on. She's breathing a little easier. Thought you would be sleeping."

"Can't sleep. Too much to think about."

"That won't help, girl, because there's no answer."

"Wrong. There's always an answer. Time will tell."

"You have a point. If we don't all die first," she sighed. "What's happened to our nice quiet family life?"

I had no answer for that. She went to her room and fell asleep almost instantly. I could hear her deep, even breathing. I guess because of the nature of her profession, she had built up an immunity to the effects of sickness and death.

I didn't think I would ever fall asleep, so I sat there on my bed with my thoughts going every which way. When I could no longer bear the suspense, I decided to go and have a peek at Floss. Before I was halfway there, I heard Aunt Rose's voice slightly raised. I paused to listen.

"You're a stubborn and foolish man. Wat it goin' tek fa you to come to yur senses an' face facts. De death of yur whole family?"

"You outta your mind, woman. Who would want to kill my family?"

"Question is who would want to kill your dogs?' Aunt Rose shot back. "Dem poor, innocent animals dat was only doin' dem job."

"Maybe the 'duppy' you all been talking about."

"You t'ink it's a joke, eh?" Aunt Rose was angry. "A duppy is one ting, dat yu can understan,' but a livin' breathin' creature is somet'ing else. Dat's where de danger is. You know, man, you should tek a good look at yur life. Somebody out to destroy you any way dey can, an' it don't matter who or what get in the way. Ah wonder if you pause to consider dat it coulda been de house with de children inside dat was set on fire? Maybe dat was jus' a warning."

I cringed as I waited for the angry outburst that I expected would follow that speech, but to my surprise, none came. Had my aunt finally managed to reach him or had he decided to ignore her? There was no way to tell. I returned to my room, waited a few minutes, and came out again, walking slowly. Father was standing looking down at Floss. I walked up to them. She looked so still. I could feel my anger rising once more.

"Think she'll make it, sir?"

He shook his head. "Hard to tell. We just have to wait and see."

At least, I consoled myself that she was still breathing. I bent and stroked her head and hoped for the best.

Aunt Rose had brewed some coffee and when I joined her in the kitchen, she offered me a cup. Father came in and he also had a cup. We sat silently. No one seemed inclined to speak, although there were many questions I wished to ask. I just could not get them out. One thing alone was clear. The puzzle we had been trying so hard to solve had, without a doubt, become even more complicated.

CHAPTER 14

The rays of the rising sun were filtering through the slats of the jalousies, sending shafts of light to various points on the wall across the room when I awoke with a thumping heart from a horrible nightmare. It involved my mother in a vague way. I tried to recall the exact sequence but failed. The only thing that etched itself in my mind was the way she kept fading away every time I tried to reach her on a lonely stretch of road, and how much she cried.

How strange, I thought. I'd never seen my mother cry in real life. What could it mean?

Memories of the tragedy of the previous night and the gruesome scene flashed through my mind. My heart leaped. I got out of bed as if propelled, slipped on my robe and ran to the kitchen. No one was about.

I looked at Floss; she was lying in a different position. I softly called her name but got no response. I called again, a little louder and lightly touched her flank with my toe. She opened her eyes and looked up at me without moving and promptly went back to sleep. I didn't know what it meant but it lifted my spirit.

Someone came in through the back door, and without looking, I knew it was my father.

He cleaned his boots noisily on the mat by the door before coming to stand beside me.

"Any movement?"

I told him the little that I had seen. He bent over her and rubbed her side and was rewarded when Floss raised her head at the sound of his voice and swished her tail just once as if to say "thank you."

"I think she'll make it," Father said.

I needed to hear that and was thankful. I took a deep breath and slowly exhaled. Without another word, I started to move away but stopped when Father, without looking at me, asked about Mama He sounded embarrassed.

"She's better." I felt uncomfortable.

"How much better?" He wanted to know. I told him the way it was. He looked doubtful.

"Girl, you sure you're telling me the truth?"

"I'm telling you the truth, sir."

"So, what do I do now?"

"I don't know, sir. I...I...I'll find out."

"I hope it won't take forever," was all he said. I guess he had finally accepted the fact that there was no point in arguing. Later that morning, Paul, Janet, and I accompanied him to a far corner of our property where we buried the dogs. He indulged us while we performed a short ceremony. We then picked bunches of wildflowers and strewed them on the graves.

Nothing much was said on our way back to the house. Janet wanted to know if animals went to heaven like people do. Paul thought she was silly. Father said that he didn't think so, and I...well, who really knew what happens after death? Any kind of death, for that matter.

Andy had declined the invitation to go with us. I could still see the scared look on his face. I had noticed, too, that he avoided getting too close to Floss or even looking at her.

No one knew exactly what he was feeling, or what his fears were since he refused to talk about his experience. We knew nothing beyond what he had told James and me. Any attempt at questioning him met with irritation and further withdrawal. It then dawned on me that there probably was something I could do to bring him some cheer. But, before making a commitment, I would first discuss it with Aunt Rose.

When we entered the passageway, Floss struggled up to greet us, her legs wobbly. She took a few faltering steps, found it too much and lay down again, rested her head on her fore paws and looked up at us with sad eyes. My heart went out to her.

Aunt Rose had placed food and water for the dog but she had, so far, only lapped up some of the water. I moved the bowl over to where she was now resting. Father patted her and expressed his opinion that although he now felt that she would recover, there was the possibility of some permanent damage. I refrained from asking what he thought it might be. I told myself it was best not to know.

Father left us, taking Paul with him, to start repairing the storeroom and save what they could of the grain. I waited until I heard hammering before I took Aunt Rose aside. I told her what I had in mind. She seemed dubious at first, but after explaining what I hoped to accomplish, she agreed that it might be a good idea after all. Phyl, on her way out to work, found us talking and wanted to know what we were discussing so secretly. She, too, expressed doubt as to the wisdom of such a move.

"From the way you describe the wild behavior of those people, I don't think you should expose these children to it. It might scare them to death." she said, frowning. "Besides, I don't think I would be comfortable with it either."

"That only happens twice a day, mid-morning and in the evening," I informed them. "We could go after lunch."

"Well...If you're quite sure, we could try." She still sounded doubtful. She turned to our aunt. "What do you think, Aunt Rose?"

"I was feelin' same as you, but if it's as Adelene say, then we could tek de chance."

"When're you thinking of going back. I really would love to see Mama."

"Tomorrow." I felt good again.

"Perfect. I'll be off tomorrow, so let's do it." Phyl clapped her hands joyfully together and shook them. "It's high time."

"Only thing," I said, frowning. "Father may not like it."

"Ugh, don't worry 'bout him," Aunt Rose said. "Jus' leave him to me."

Phyl and I both laughed. That was our Aunt Rose, a staunch ally. Phyl told us not to expect her back until the next morning as she was scheduled to work through the night.

I asked Aunt Rose not to tell Mama of our plan. It was to be a surprise. She promised to keep our secret. I said nothing to the others. I didn't want to create too much excitement by building up their expectations for too long a time. I thought the next morning would be time enough.

So it was that with much rejoicing all five of us left next day to visit our mother. The look of joy on her face when she saw us was one that would remain etched in my memory forever. For the first time, I saw tears in her eyes, but I knew they were tears of happiness. At that moment, I felt so happy that I, too, felt like crying. I moved away in order to compose myself.

Just seeing Mama and knowing for sure that she was alright had transformed everyone to such a degree that I was amazed.

A few minutes with her and Andy had pulled right out of his shell. Paul was all smiles and he was chatting away at such a speed that even I couldn't match. Well, Phyl, she just sat there looking so pleased.

Although I had cautioned them not to talk about the fire, Janet, unable to contain herself, blurted it out before anyone could stop her. I gave her a warning look but she rushed right on with the rest of the story. Mama's look of alarm made me want to grab my little sister and shake her. Phyl did what she could to soften things, but the damage was done. Mama's mood changed.

She looked worried.

"I want you all to be careful," she said solemnly. "Very, very careful." We assured her that we would.

"When 're you coming home, ma'am?" Paul asked.

"Soon, son." She looked at each of us in turn. "I'm making some plans. You'll all have to prepare yourself for a change. In life, sometimes things happen that we have no control over, and we're forced to do things we really don't want to do jus' to put them right. I won't say anymore right now, but I don't want you all to worry. Understand?"

Phyl and I exchanged glances. The others mumbled in the affirmative although I felt sure they, like myself, had no idea what she meant. No point in asking questions. We would get no answer until she thought the time was right. Mama, obviously aware of our confusion, hurriedly changed the subject by asking the one question she had so far avoided.

"How's your father?"

"Father's fine, Mama. You don't have to worry about him," Phyl said.

"Not worrying," Mama said. She pursed her lips and looked everywhere but at us. Once again, she changed the subject. This time it was to inquire of the three younger ones how they were doing in school. They all said they were studying hard, and Mama seemed satisfied until Janet, the great chatterbox, informed her that Andy had missed some days from school. Now I really felt like shaking her real hard.

Mama looked fixedly at me.

"And why would he be out of school?"

"He was sick, Mama. Sick in the hospital."

"Oh, dear Father in Heaven! What is this? Why would he be in the hospital?" she asked with deep anxiety.

"He...."

"Shut up, Janet!" I snapped. "Why you talk so?"

"What you all hiding?" Mama asked suspiciously.

"Nothing, Mama." Phyl came to my rescue. "He had a fall and got a bad cut on his arm. It had to be stitched."

I fervently hoped that would satisfy her and we would not have to reveal everything.

"Come here. Let me see." Andy drew closer to her and rolled up his sleeve to show his arm that was still bandaged for the stitches had not yet been removed.

"That's bad, eh?" she touched it gingerly. "You have a lot of pain?"

"No, ma'am. It's getting better."

"But how...?" Mercifully, she was stopped from asking the question that I felt sure would put us on the spot.

"Well, well, such a nice little gathering." "Mother" Robinson was standing by the door with a radiant smile. " All these children yours, Mrs. Bailey?"

"Oh, yes," Mama beamed and proudly pointed us out "That's Phyllis, my oldest girl. Adelene you know already, then Paul, Andrew, and Janet, the youngest. The first is a boy named James."

"Lovely children, something to be proud of." "Mother" said, studying each of us in turn.

Then her gaze remained fixed on Andy. "Mrs. Bailey, I see you named the boys from the Bible. Why not the girls?"

"You know that just happen. It wasn't a plan." Mama responded, looking thoughtful.

"Well, that was good, very good." "Mother" was still studying Andy. Suddenly, she shivered, sucked in her breath, and closed her eyes. My heart thumped. When she opened her eyes, she was again looking at Andy. She held out a hand to him.

"Come here, sonny." Andy gave her a scared look and drew closer to Mama.

"Go to her, son. She won't hurt you." Mama urged him on by giving him a gentle push.

Andy reluctantly obeyed. He moved haltingly to stand in front of "Mother," who took him by the shoulders and slowly turned him around three times. Then with him facing us, she laid a hand on his head, and stretched the other out to us and began to pray that we would all be divinely protected and healed, ending with a torrent of the unknown tongue. I felt myself blush. It always made me feel uncomfortable. Although I wouldn't say it to anyone, I thought of it as a whole lot of gibberish. I dared not look at Phyl. Instead, I averted my eyes for fear that my thoughts could be read by this woman who seemed able to peer into the souls of others.

She had healed Mama, by whatever means, from a baffling illness. It was obvious that she had also sensed something unusual about Andy. There was no doubt in my mind that the gift she possessed was of a power beyond herself and she was specially chosen to use it as an instrument of good. Whatever it was would remain beyond my comprehension, but my family would forever owe her a debt of gratitude.

I forced myself to look up. "Mother" was still holding Andy, who looked more relaxed.

She patted his head and gently shoved him back to us.

"You're a good boy," she said and turned to Mama. "Mrs. Bailey, you are blessed in having such children. I wish you all well." Mama beamed with pride. At that moment, for the first time since all our troubles began, I saw my mother the way she used to be. It made me feel very happy.

Saying goodbye to her was no easy matter. None of us really wanted to leave her. After about the third or fourth attempt, we finally made it. As soon as we were safely away from the boundaries of the property where the Mission stood, I was faced with a barrage of questions.

Who was that woman? Why was she dressed that way? What was the strange language she spoke? Was she a foreigner? Why did she do what she did to Andy? Why...why...? I did my best to answer what I could. The rest I truthfully said I didn't know. They gave up after a while, not completely satisfied, but a much happier group than when we had left home. Paul, Andy, and Janet walked ahead, slowing down every now and then when either one saw something that attracted their attention. Phyl and I moved silently along at a slower pace. I wondered how she felt about the whole experience. I wasn't too anxious to find out knowing what a great skeptic she was about such things.

"Well, Adelene," Phyl broke the silence. I braced myself. "I must say that you've made a believer out of me. Despite what you said, I never expected to see that much of a change. Thank God you didn't listen to me."

Was I hearing right? I looked at her and saw how serious she had become and said, "The person to thank in all honesty is Katherine, and we must always remember that."

166

"I don't think that will be easy to forget." She didn't sound pleased. "I only hope she don't hold it over us."

"What you mean by that?" I asked sharply, feeling deep resentment.

"Well, you know, she may start acting uppity because she knows so much."

"Woman, get off your high horse!" I snapped."You think you better than her?"

"I didn't say that."

"Soun' so to me."

"I just mean that..."

I covered my ears and said sternly, "I don't want to hear. Katherine is not that kind of person."

"Okay, okay, sorry." She'd raised her voice. I released my ears and scowled at her.

"Shame on you."

She shrugged, then chuckled. "You should've seen your face." I couldn't help smiling. "Mama's really looking good to me." Phyl said after we had sobered up. "Why do you think she's still staying on there?"

"Maybe she's makin' sure."

"That's a strange place, you get the feeling you're in another world. Weird."

I knew exactly what she meant. I wondered how she would have reacted had she witnessed one of their rituals.

"You get used to it," I said, conscious that I wasn't being entirely truthful.

"I suppose." She shrugged again, then said musingly. "She's not the same."

"Who? Mama?"

"Yes, something's different about her, can't say exactly what."

I was surprised. I had not seen any change. But maybe seeing her as often as I did, somehow it had eluded me.

"Well," I felt uncertain. "After her experience anything is possible."

"Hmm. It could be temporary, though."

"Hope you're right."

Ahead of us, the others had settled to a slower pace. Janet looked tired. It was a long journey for a small child. I called a halt and suggested we take turns carrying her, but Paul volunteered to take her the rest of the way. Riding piggy-back, she kept looking back from time to time to see if Andy was following. He stopped abruptly as we neared the gate. Janet looked back and saw him.

"Come on!" she called in her bossiest voice. He did not respond. She started fidgeting and Paul lowered her to the ground. Andy hadn't moved. She ran to him and grabbed his hand.

"Come on." He pulled his hand away and she flounced off, her head held high. When Phyl and I reached Andy, he was just standing there, staring ahead.

"What happen, Andy?" I touched his shoulder. Without looking around, he gripped my arm and held on tightly. I looked at Phyl, but she was paying no attention to us. Something had attracted her attention. I saw nothing. I began to feel the eerie tingling sensation that had become so familiar to me since all our troubles began. I assumed an air of bravado for Andy's sake. The minute we passed through the gate, he let go of my arm and made a mad dash up the path to the house.

"What's the matter with that boy?" I tried to laugh but failed.

"Don't ask," Phyl said in a hushed tone. "I feel like doing the same thing myself."

"What?" I looked at her, saw the look on her face and fear took complete control of me.

With a loud whoop, I leaped forward at my fastest pace. Phyl followed suit and together we burst into the drawing room, slammed the door shut and collapsed out of breath on the settee.

"Wat's dis, wat's dis?" Aunt Rose came hurrying in. "You all come in like some demon chasin' yu."

"Close enough, Aunt Rose." Phyl said, and we started to giggle. Aunt Rose eyed us suspiciously, shook her head, then turned abruptly and left us.

When we had sufficiently recovered, I tried to get Phyl to tell me what we had run from, but she said it was best if I didn't know. I kept at her but she was adamant. I gave up. She was probably right. I had enough to contend with as it was.

I forgot everything when the gnawing in my stomach made me head for the kitchen.

Phyl followed close behind. I was surprised to see a young man seated at the table, a large brown cap covering one knee. He stared at us. Then slowly, he let his eyes rove over Phyl, then me.

I felt myself blush.

"Who are you?" Phyl asked haughtily.

"Dat's Lester," Aunt Rose said before he could answer. "Yur father hire him to keep watch 'round here."

"A good idea." Phyl looked thoughtful. "Well, Lester, I hope you're up to the job."

"Ah hope so too, Miss." He had a deep, flat voice.

I turned away for the simple reason that he made me feel uncomfortable. Besides, I had Floss on my mind. She was not in sight. Had she succumbed after all? I was afraid to ask.

"She's outside, so don't kill yur'self." It was Aunt Rose. I was unaware that she was watching me, and had guessed at my thoughts. I exhaled the breath I was not even conscious of holding and gave her a teary smile, overwhelmed by the wave of emotion that had enveloped me. I guess I was tired and still so afraid. To cover up, I rushed to help her get the meal that she had prepared for us on the table.

That was all it took for me to compose myself. I must confess that it was one of the most delicious meals I ever had, and I complemented Aunt Rose, effusively, on her skill. She brushed it aside, but I could tell by the expression on her face that she was very pleased.

As soon as we were done eating and everything washed and stored away, I called Paul and asked him to accompany me outside. I had half expected him to refuse but he complied without question. Floss was lying in the shade of a mango tree. When she heard us, she got up and came to meet us, wagging her tail. She was still a bit wobbly but definitely on the mend.

She nuzzled us and we both patted her.

"You goin' leave her out here tonight?" Paul asked with concern.

"No way." I undid her leash. "I'm taking her back inside right now."

"Good. They could come back and try to kill her again."

"Right."

But who, I wondered, *were they?*

CHAPTER 15

Lester took up his vigil in the storeroom that night for what would probably be an indefinite period. Whether or not he was capable of effectively performing his duty remained to be seen. In the meantime, I, for one, felt safer just knowing he was there.

I'd hoped to talk privately with Aunt Rose before retiring, but the opportunity did not arise. Even after everyone had settled in for the night, I could not take the chance since, for obvious reasons, Father stayed home. I felt sure that she would have been able to shed some light on the little speech Mama had made to us.

What were the changes she had planned? How would they affect us?

Mama always told me that I worried too much about things. I had to admit she was right as I lay in the dark, thinking of all the possibilities. I fell asleep still wondering.

I was awakened far into the night from a deep sleep by the sound that always sent chills up my spine. Father had wanted to put Floss back outside on the porch, but I had timidly asked if he could allow her to stay inside for just another night, at least. He relented, which surprised me, but I was too glad to even question his motive. Now I wished he had insisted as I listened to the hoarse, mournful howls emanating from Floss.

I thought of Mama. Had she suffered a relapse? Would she die after all? What of the rest of us? Were we really safe? These thoughts churned through my mind fueled by deep-rooted superstitions that were so much a part of our cultural heritage. Someone was going to die. Someone we knew from the district. It had been proven time and again. Just as the screeching of an owl heralded in new life.

I knew Floss had to be put out, but I did not have the courage to do it alone. While I lay there pondering, I heard Janet call from across the room in a frightened whisper.

"Adelene?"

"Yes?"

"Can I come in your bed?"

"Yes," I said after a brief hesitation. She scrambled across, climbed on the bed and quickly pulled the cover over her head as she snuggled up against me. *My feelings exactly,* I thought., but I would never let her know that I, too, was afraid.

Someone was moving about. Then I heard the muffled sound of my father's voice. A door slammed and I breathed a sigh of relief. I knew that there was now no question of Floss ever staying inside again. I lay awake in a tormented state until all became quiet. A quiet that brought no comfort, just a sadness that I couldn't quite explain.

Sleep eluded me for the rest of the night. I was feeling battered and sluggish when I dragged myself out of bed next morning. I was both mentally and physically drained. I couldn't recall ever being that way before. Thankfully, Aunt Rose was up before everyone and had made breakfast.

When I arrived, she was dishing up a generous portion for Lester. She gave me a searching look, but said nothing. Considering the way I felt, I was glad as I was in no mood to talk. I filled a large mug with coffee and shuffled back to my room. I knew how strongly Mama disapproved of any kind of food or drink being consumed in areas other than those designed for such things except, of course, in cases of sickness, but I could not tolerate being subjected to the insolent stare of that young man.

The coffee revived me. I got Janet up for school. I was putting the finishing touches to her hair when Phyl came in and announced that she was taking Andy to the hospital to have the stitches removed. By the time I returned to the kitchen, Lester had already left.

Paul, all ready for school, was having breakfast. He urged Janet to hurry so they wouldn't be late. It was still not a good time to talk with Aunt Rose. It seemed that the opportunity would never present itself in view of the fact that she would be leaving for her home soon. I decided to let the matter rest, and it was only then that I noticed that Aunt Rose, who was normally effusive, was acting out of character. Did it have anything to do with the visit Mama had so urgently wanted her to make? The more I thought about it, the more convinced I became.

"Adelene.'

I jumped. "Eh, eh."

"You so far away, wat you t'inking 'bout so hard, Chile?" Aunt Rose eyed me keenly.

"Oh...nothin,' ma'am" I pulled myself together.

"Let me tell you something, Chile, one pound of fret won't pay a ounce of debt. So jus' take t'ings easy, eh?"

"I know, Aunt Rose."

Paul and Janet said goodbye, and we were left alone.

"Yu mus' take some extra clothes for yur modder today." Aunt Rose continued. "Ah'm not coming back here after today to stay, because between yur father an' that young man you all should be safe enough. I'll drop in from time to time to see how you all doin'"

"But why...?" I began.

"Ah have to leave now," she said quickly. "Ah'll see you later."

I knew when to shut up. It didn't take a genius to figure that something was afoot. Something that she did not want to discuss with me. I became suspicious about the extra clothing she wanted me to take to Mama. Why was it necessary?

In my anxiety, I left everything as it was in the kitchen, hurriedly collected an assortment of apparel from my mother's wardrobe, and left the house.

I could see right away that I had wasted precious hours the night before worrying about Mama. She could not have looked better. She took one look at me, saw how out of breath I was and ordered me to sit down. She handed me a glass of water from which I took a few sips. I placed my elbows on my thighs, cupped my face in my hands and stayed that way until I regained my equilibrium.

"Now, tell me, what do you get from working yourself up like this?" There was no reproach in her tone.

I shook my head, too choked up to speak.

"When're you going to learn that to be calm is to be strong? To panic about anything, you lose your ability to think with a clear head and you end up doing foolish things. There will always be problems, but the way you solve them depends on the way you approach them. Remember that, Adelene."

"I'll remember," I said, abashed. She patted my shoulder then took a deep breath.

I braced myself.

"The other day I mention to all of you that there would be some changes," she began. "I wasn't quite sure if what I had in mind would work out so I had a talk with my sister about it, and we agree that after I leave here, I would go and stay with her for a while."

"But why, Mama?" I tried to be calm.

"There are forces at work battling against me and I have no desire to take up the fight at this time. I just need to be by myself to work things out to my satisfaction."

I couldn't pretend that I did not understand, but I was so disappointed that I couldn't think of anything more to say.

"In all the years I've been married to your father," Mama continued. with a far-away look, "I devoted every minute of my time making a good home for my family and I've been a faithful wife and mother, and I believe I deserve the consideration and respect that go with it."

There was just a hint of bitterness in her tone. I knew for her to express that much meant there were other things she was suppressing.

"How...long you goin' to stay at Aunt Rose's, ma'am?"

"Right now I can't say. It depends on a lot of things. I know I can rely on you to run the house, so I'm leaving it up to you. The other children can stop by every day after school to see me if they'd like to, so that I can stay in close touch with them."

"But what about Father?" I burst out.

"He'll understand, believe me, so don't you worry." She said it as if it didn't matter at all.

I gazed at her in wonder. This was too much. Phyl was right. She had changed! But where was it taking us? Whatever the outcome, I had to trust her judgment. But I realized that after all she'd said, the only thing that was clear to me was the fact that she would not be returning home right away.

The feelings of anxiety with which I had arrived were now being replaced by a slow-burning anger. Why couldn't she tell me the whole truth so I could understand? I was tired of speculating. Tired of being treated like a little child after all we'd been through. She had considered me mature enough to assume the responsibility of running the house, but not to be taken fully into her confidence.

I excused myself to go outside and cool off. She called after me not to stay out too long, but I pretended not to hear. The yard was deserted. Everyone was no doubt resting and conserving their strength for the rigors of the midday meeting. I moved aimlessly around, fuming at what I considered unfair treatment. I told myself I had a right to know everything.

Every right in the world.

"A young, pretty face like yours shouldn't be wearing such a deep frown." The voice startled me. It was "Mother" Robinson. I'd been walking with my head down and had not seen her where she sat on a bench in the shade of a tree. I wondered how long she had been observing me.

"Come and sit here," she invited, patting the vacant part of the bench. I obeyed, feeling somewhat ill at ease.

"If you want to talk, I'll listen," she said, "and I'll help if I can."

I didn't know what to say to her. She would probably laugh at me if I told her the reason I was disgruntled. So I asked instead if the problem that had brought Mama to her, would recur. She pondered the question before answering.

"If a man let himself fall into the same ditch twice, he is a fool, for the knowledge he gained from the first fall should have given him enough wisdom to avoid the second fall." She paused and smiled "I don't think your mother is a fool."

"That's why she's not coming home, 'Mother'?"

She shook her head. "No... I think it's personal, but it's not for me to say. It wasn't easy going through all that she did. So be patient; you will know it all in time."

My anger had dissipated and I was able to smile.

When I had first met her, I was struck by how refined she looked and the proper manner in which she spoke. Her English was never broken and she always maintained her dignity. It was out of keeping with the way she lived and the work she performed. So, one day, out of curiosity, I had asked Katherine what she knew about "Mother" and was shocked to learn that she was from a prominent family and had been studying law when she was converted, or as Katherine put it, "got the call." It was rumored that her family after trying unsuccessfully to get her back on track, had finally given up and disowned her. I remember how sad it had made me feel. But as I looked at her now, I could see that she was content to be who she was.

"I have to get back to Mama," I said, rising and smoothing down my skirt. I held out a hand to her and she clasped it warmly. "Thank you for everything."

"I have to see your mother, so we'll go together. We have some arrangements to make."

Mama was dressed and waiting for me. I felt guilty about the way I had been feeling earlier, but if she was aware of it, she gave no sign.

It was arranged that "Mother" Robinson would visit our home in two days so that the house and grounds could be consecrated. My job was to make sure there were no obstacles in the way. I did not anticipate any problems since the visit was arranged for a time when everyone was expected to be out, with the possible exception of Phyl.

Although the events of the past weeks had shaken her unbelief somewhat, Phyl still harbored a fair amount of skepticism. I could only guess at what her reaction would be to this latest development, but I was confident she could be relied upon to cooperate.

It was time to say goodbye to this good woman who had made such a difference in our lives. I knew I would never forget her. She had earned a special place in my heart.

For the second time in days, I saw a glitter of tears in my mother's eyes and I could only guess at the waves of emotion that put them there. "Mother"

Robinson laid a hand on her shoulder and in her characteristic manner, delivered a few cryptic messages which Mama seemed to have no difficulty understanding by the way she smiled and nodded.

"Walk good," she ended. "Be wise, and God bless you all."

We thanked her again and took our leave. A few of the women who had attended Mama in one way or another were outside waiting to say goodbye and to wish her luck. Two of them promised to visit her. Mama seemed pleased by that, which surprised me knowing how much of a loner she was, and how much she valued her privacy. Had she undergone that much of a change? Only time would tell.

As we passed through the gate, I prayed that we would never have to return for a similar reason. I looked back just once to find the little group of people watching us. I waved, then kept my eyes straight ahead.

When we arrived at Aunt Rose's cottage, it was lunch time. She had a meal waiting for us. After we had eaten, we chatted for a while and I was able to fit a few more pieces of the puzzle together. Though still not enough to form a complete picture, but I was hoping to hang around long enough to learn more.

After a while, Mama paused to remind me that considering all I had to do, it was wise to make a start so that I could have things ready by the time everyone else got home. I was disappointed but I had a duty to perform.

I started for home with conflicting emotions. Knowing how anxiously everyone was looking forward to Mama's return, I hated to be the one to tell them it was not to be. Not for a while, anyway. I decided that it would be best to keep quiet about it until after they had their dinner so as not to spoil their appetites. It was a decision I never regretted when I saw all the sad faces.

I hastened to inform them that Mama had suggested that if they would like to, they could stop by each day after school to see her, so that they could keep in close touch. On hearing that, there was a remarkable change in their attitudes. But that did not stop the question for which I had no answer. It was unsettling. Secretly I wondered if, for some obscure reason, our family was in danger of breaking up. Just the thought of it aroused feelings of panic. Regardless of the outcome, nothing would ever be the same again.

CHAPTER 16

I had crossed one hurdle, but the most difficult one was ahead. I had to face my father with the latest news, and at that prospect all the old fears I'd had of approaching him regained control of me. They seemed to negate the new kinship we had shared since the night of the fire.

I became more nervous as the evening wore on. What would his reaction be? Would I be blamed for everything? He had not seen Mama since the day I boldly took her away. Still fresh in my mind was that embarrassing episode when he had tried to see her and was unceremoniously turned away. Since then, he had made a point of asking me about her every day. I had begun to get the feeling that he really loved her and was eager to see her.

I thought of soliciting Paul's aid but dismissed it as being cowardly. In the past, I'd handled worse situations with more courage. Why then was I getting worked up about something as simple as this?

I was pulled out of my reverie when Paul announced that he was going out to the backyard to while away some time. Andy stood undecided. I encouraged him to do the same, but he hung back until Janet playfully poked him in the back, urging him on. He complied somewhat reluctantly. With Janet skipping happily behind him. It was good to see them once again showing signs of normalcy.

Sounds of laughter drifted in as they played, with Janet's loud squeals dominating the others, and Floss's sharp barks adding to the din as she romped around with them. She had regained most of her strength. Father was careful to leash her at nights as a protective measure against further harm should our nocturnal visitor continue to prowl.

Although there were changes in the overall situation, things remained essentially the same. Until we discovered who our enemy or enemies were and took steps to assure our safety, we would never be free to live our lives in peace.

Suddenly, there was a loud knock on the front door. I started violently, and the dish I had been drying slipped and fell, breaking into several pieces. I moved cautiously toward the door, my arms and legs weak from nervous tension.

"Who...who's there?" I called.

"It's me, James."

I unlocked the door and let him in. He gave me a searching look.

"You okay?"

I nodded.

"You don't look so good to me."

I explained what had happened, trying to make light of it.

"Sorry," he said sympathetically.

"Don't worry, I'll be alright soon." I took a deep breath, exhaled slowly and looked him over.

"You're looking good.

"Thanks, I try my best to keep fit."

"That's smart," I said. "Glad to see you."

"Glad to see you too." He looked pensive. "I know that I should come over more often, but between the job and my family, there isn't much time left over."

He paused and cleared his throat. "I understand there was a fire?"

"Who told you?"

"I saw Phyllis yesterday at the hospital."

"Oh?" I raised my brows questioningly. "What were you doing there?"

"A student from my class had an accident in the schoolyard. I went to check on him."

"That was very nice of you. I hope it's not serious?'

"No, he'll be fine."

"Did Phyl tell you about Butch and Nipper?"

"Oh, yes. I couldn't believe it. It's hard to accept things like that, you know." He knitted his brows.

"What's really going on here, Adelene?"

"Only God knows." I could feel my anger rising at my inability to clarify matters for him. "The only thing that's clear is that we are dealing with two separate things, one natural, and the other supernatural. But I have a strong feeling that they are connected somehow. I know it sounds crazy, but I can't help it. What I'd really like to understand is why would anyone go to such extremes. What do they hope to gain?"

"It's unbelievable." James shook his head in bewilderment. "This can't go on."

"You're right about that."

"So how is it with Mama?"

"Mama is quite well, physically," I was happy to say. "She left the Mission today but she's staying with Aunt Rose for now."

"That's strange. For her to do that she must have a very good reason." James's brows furrowed. "What else can you tell me, Adelene?"

I went over everything in my mind, every little detail I could remember and recounted them to him. Only after I told him of Father's visit to the Mission and the verbal exchange that took place, did he interrupt me.

"I think I'm beginning to get the picture."

"Want to tell me?" I asked hopefully.

He was slow in replying, and when he did, it was not to my satisfaction.

"I think I'd better keep it to myself for now until I'm sure. I don't want to jump to any conclusions and find out I'm wrong."

"Just give me a hint." I coaxed, feeling more frustrated than ever at everyone's insistence at being secretive.

"Look, I...," He said no more for just then Father walked in carrying a small package. He was accompanied by a gentleman by the name of Porter, one of our neighbors, who lived a half a mile or so from us. We rarely had visitors. Usually Father did his socializing away from home, so I figured there had to be a special purpose for this visit.

"Well, James, how's life treating you?" Father asked after the usual greeting. He sounded cheerful.

"Very good, sir. How about you?"

"Oh, so-so." He clapped a heavy hand on James's shoulder. "You keep up the good work, son."

"I'll try."

"We're goin' to have a drink. Want one?"

"No, thank you." James shook his head and smiled. "My stomach can't take that hard stuff."

I suppressed a smile at the excuse. I knew only too well that he dared not go home to his wife with liquor reeking on his breath.

"Oh, well, you must know," Father said as he turned to me. "Adelene, please bring me a couple of glasses."

As I hurried to get them, I remembered the message I had to deliver. It was not a matter to discuss in the presence of a stranger and I prayed he would leave soon. I needed to get it over with as soon as possible. When I returned with the glasses, I ventured to ask Father if he would like to have his dinner first.

"Later," he said.

I went outside to remind the others that it was time to settle down and do their homework. There was some resistance, but they finally gave in. I made sure they were fully settled before attending to the rest of my chores.

As I moved about, I could hear snatches of the conversation among the men. Enough to conclude that a plan was being worked out to set a trap for whoever was terrorizing us. I became so excited I wished I could have been a part of it. I began to fantasize ways in which I could participate. I was having so much fun that I started to chuckle.

"What are you thinking about that's so funny?" James demanded. I hadn't heard him come in.

"Don't ask." I said lightly with the grin still on my face. "You leaving now?"

"Yes, I want to stop by Aunt Rose's. I long to see Mama."

"She'll be very glad to see you, too."

"I know."

After he left, I went to my room to rest but ended up helping Janet with her homework. When it was done, I flung myself across my bed, hoping our visitor would soon leave. Before I knew it, I was sound asleep.

I was walking along a winding path through the greenest cornfield I'd ever seen. There was a cool breeze rippling through the leaves and I could smell the fresh earth recently mound around the roots to help stimulate growth. I felt lighthearted. Suddenly, I became aware of a presence and my whole being tingled with fear. I looked behind me and saw a large dog moving toward me. Its eyes glowing eerily in the gloom. I tried to run but made little progress. Somehow, I reached a clearing, from which stretched a wide paved road. I knew I had to get on to that road because it would take me to my mother and safety. I tried to get to it but it kept moving. Instead, I found myself facing a steep, rocky hill. The animal was getting closer. In desperation I took a flying leap onto the rocks and pulled my legs up just in time to escape the wildly snapping jaws of the animal.

"Adelene! Adelene!" Someone was calling to me from somewhere far away.

"Adelene, wake up, wake up!"

I opened my eyes in a daze. A dark figure was standing over me, shaking me. "Wake up!"

"Yeees." My mind was still muddled and my heart pounding. I felt faint.

"You 'wake?" It was Phyl. She put the light on and stood looking down at me with concern.

"Please get some water for me," I whispered.

She hurried out. I was confused. What was she doing here? I had no idea what time it was, only that it was night. I was still fully clothed.

Phyl returned with the water. I sat up and looked dazedly around.

"Sip it slowly." she warned. "That was some nightmare you had. You were making some straaange sounds."

"Yes?" I managed at last. "Your dog attacked me in my sleep."

"You're joking," she chuckled.

I shook my head. "What's the time?"

"Eight o'clock."

"How come you're home?"

She looked embarrassed. "They run me out the hospital, said I was overdoing it. Which is true, but I couldn't tell them I was afraid to come home in the night."

"You come alone?"

"No, had company right to the door."

I closed my eyes. I was still not feeling so good. Waking up so suddenly and all. Phyl suggested I get up and change for bed. I wanted to have a talk with her, but I didn't have the energy. Instead, I pulled myself together just long enough to change, and then I went right back to sleep.

Father was already up and about when I went to start breakfast next morning. I didn't waste any time speculating but blurted out the facts and waited for an outburst. When none came, I sneaked a look at him. He was just standing there with a tight look on his face, then he turned abruptly and went outside.

I busied myself and tried not to think too much of his behavior. When he returned, he maintained his silence. I soon realized that he was more disturbed than I could ever have imagined. He had only a cup of coffee and left the rest of his breakfast untouched. On his way out again, he hesitated briefly at the door to ask, "When did she say she want to see me?"

"Any time, sir," I hastened to say.

He left.

Thank God that was over. The fireworks that I had been bracing myself for did not happen.

Later that morning, while Phyl and I were out shopping, we talked at length. I learned she had applied for vacation and would be at home the next couple weeks.

"And," she said with an air of mystery, "I finally decided to go through with the wedding."

"About time." I felt happy for her. "When're you going to do it?"

"I'll decide as soon as I talk it over with Mama."

Things were looking up. The only thing left now was the hope that the cloud that still overshadowed us would be completely obliterated by then.

The town was unusually quiet. We didn't run into anyone we knew, which pleased me enormously. I really was not inclined to answer anyone's probing questions about our affairs. In a district the size of ours, news had a way of spreading with incredible speed.

When we returned home, I was still feeling energetic, so I left Phyl to put away the groceries and went outside to help Katherine with the laundry. She was rinsing and wringing each piece by hand. I would then take them and pin them on the clothesline to dry.

I told her about my dream.

"Well," she began in her usual down-to-earth manner. "De fac' dat Miss Liz get ridda her problem don't mean dat everyt'ing alright, you know. You all mus' look 'bout de nex' part an dat's something entirely different."

"Like what?" I knew instantly that it was the wrong question.

"Adelene, use yur head!" she said crossly. "Who set de fire? Tell me dat."

When I didn't answer, she went on. "The only way dat could happen is if somebody like you an' me do it. Ah doan know if you know any duppy dat can strike matches."

It was hilarious the way she said it. I burst out laughing hysterically. Katherine kept a straight face while she watched me wipe the tears from my eyes.

"Sweet you, eh?" she said and continued with her work. "One ting you mus' know, Ah can't help you no more."

That sobered me and I continued helping her in thoughtful silence. I didn't know it then, but fate was just ready to lend us a helping hand.

Paul, Andy, and Janet went to visit Mama and that threw everything off schedule. It was almost dusk when they came hurrying in holding hands. It made me mad that they had to feel so afraid.

Father arrived soon after, once again accompanied by Mr. Porter, and one of his sons who was about Phyl's age. It was quite obvious that they meant business. Father shared his meal with them, and after they had finished eating, they all went out to join Lester.

I would have given anything to know what strategy they had worked out, but there was no chance of that.

Paul wanted to know the reason for the unusual activity. He became quite excited when I told him and wanted to rush right out to join them. It took some doing, but I managed to convince him that it would be foolish to go barging in. There was no telling what mood Father was in. Paul fidgeted around the kitchen and I had the feeling that if I had turned my back, he would have sneaked out.

Father came in to ask me to make coffee. Lots of it. Paul seized the opportunity to make his request. As I thought, Father refused. He explained that he could not risk putting Paul in danger, for it was a man's job. Paul fumed, echoing the same words I had used when I thought I was not being treated like an adult. I sympathized with him. After a while, Phyl came in and managed to calm him down and he sulked off to bed.

While I set up the coffee for the men, Phyl prepared some snacks just in case they might be needed.

In the meantime, we talked more candidly than we ever had before. It helped us to get a better understanding of each other. We hung around as long as we could then finally went off to bed. I snuggled in and fell asleep almost instantly.

It couldn't have been too long after when I was awakened by loud noises coming from outside.

Someone was shouting, "Hold him, hold him! Don't let him get away." Other voices were joining in.

I sprang out of bed and slipped on a dress in record time. Throwing caution to the wind, I ran outside, following the sounds. I stopped a safe distance from where I could just make out the men struggling with their victim.

"Tie him up," someone said. Whoever they had caught was not making it easy for them.

"Lester, get a light, quick!" It was my father's voice.

As Lester scooted back to the storeroom, I watched as they wound a rope around the man they were holding.

"What's happening?" Phyl's voice came at me from the dark. She was breathing hard.

"Seems like they catch Mr. Whoever."

Lester returned carrying a lantern. Phyl and I crept a little closer for a better look. The light was held high to reveal the man's face. He held his head high, defiantly. I gasped.

"You? Elliston?" Father sounded really shocked. "My God!"

"What God?" the man asked scornfully. "What the hell you know about God, you stinking home-wrecker!"

"And whose home am I supposed to be wrecking?"

"Mine!" the man said vehemently. "Mine!"

"So with that belief you decide to sneak 'round my property like a common thief in the night and create havoc?"

"Yes!" Mr. Elliston yelled defiantly. He struggled against his restraint. Although he was a large man, at the moment he was helpless. "You not satisfied with what you got, you mus' take what another man have as well. I inten' to kill you an' your whole damn family. You son of a b----, but this is not the end of it. You not goin' mess with me life an' upset me home an get away wit' it. Never! Ah die first!"

"You're a madman," Father growled "You don't know what the hell you're saying."

"But you know," the man said. "You know exactly what Ah talkin' about. You foolin' 'round with me wife. You turn her against me."

"No man who considers himself a real man need accuse another of stealing his wife," Father shot at him. "You consider yourself a man, Elliston?"

"More than you could ever be," was the wrathful response.

"Then what do you have to worry about?"

The man strained once more to release himself, but not only was he bound, he was firmly held by three pairs of hands.

"Wat you goin' do wit' him, sah?" Lester asked excitedly.

"I have a mind to give him a good thrashing he'll never forget. But I'm going to let the fool go," Father growled.

I wondered why he was being so generous.

"But, sah, him will come back and do the same t'ing again." Lester protested, and the other men agreed.

"Maybe, but he's not worth getting you all and myself in trouble with the law," Father explained. "If he's wise, he won't come back. I'm going to make sure of that, and if he should try again, he'll end up with a bullet in his gut." This last statement was uttered with deadly calm.

"You think you can frighten me?" Mr. Elliston asked. "You think I'm 'fraid of you?"

"I want no man to fear me," Father said. "You're an evil man. Get outta here before I change my mind."

I was shocked. Was that my father talking like that? All this time, Phyl and I had watched silently. I whispered to her that we should get away before anyone saw us. I was battling with so many emotions, the deepest of which was shame. Shame that my father could be accused of such a thing.

We didn't wait to hear or see more. We hurried back inside and ended up in her room, where we sat in silence for a while until I broke it.

"Phyl, do you think what that man said is true?" Even as I asked, I knew how hypocritical it was.

She shrugged. "I heard rumors," was all she said.

"You never said anything," I accused.

"I had no proof. And you know how I feel about gossip."

"But this is a family matter!" I snapped, irked by her attitude.

"So, now you know."

But hadn't I guessed it all along? Why had I fought so hard to repress it?

Simple, I did not want it to be true. Memories came flooding back. Things said, things seen, things heard since the day of Mrs. Bowen's visit. All leading to the same conclusion Now it was all very clear.

CHAPTER 17

"**M**other" Robinson and two of her followers arrived at our home at precisely nine o'clock next morning. She was dressed in ordinary clothes. I had never seen her without her religious garb before, and was pleasantly surprised to see the difference it made. She was, indeed, a very attractive woman.

At her request, I guided her through the house to acquaint her with the layout. Special interest was shown in our parents' bedroom. As soon as that was over, Phyl and I left them to their work.

With time on our hands, I suggested we go egg hunting. Some of our laying hens had rejected the ready-made coop and had made nests for themselves in out-of-the-way places. Phyl thought it was a good idea, so I got a small basket and we started out. Although I suspected that the incident the night before was uppermost in her mind as it was on mine, we both avoided any mention of it.

That morning, I had been unable to look at my father because the embarrassment was too great. I wondered if he had any idea that we had witnessed the whole scene. He had eaten very little and said even less. I was very relieved when he went off to work.

After searching around, we found four nests. A hen was already sitting on the first but from the others, we collected over a dozen eggs, still fresh. We walked aimlessly around, to kill time, until Phyl asked, "What you suppose they're doing in the house?"

"I don't really know how, but the idea is to drive out any evil spirit that's around."

"You really believe all that stuff, Adelene?" Her tone lacked the usual skepticism, but had a need to be assured.

My hesitation was brief.

"Yes...like you I had a lotta doubts, but I've seen too much to hold on to them."

"I can understand that."

We walked on until we reached the clearing where the dogs were buried. I pointed it out to Phyl. The wildflowers had all dried up and grass was springing up on the mounds.

Impulsively, I gathered more flowers and strewed them on. Phyl laughingly said I was being overly sentimental. I didn't agree with her. She may have been moved more than she cared to admit, for as we retraced our steps, she asked how I felt about going to see our mother after the women had left. I agreed it would be a great idea.

The three women were now moving about the yard and we stopped to watch them as they looked around. When they stopped, we moved to join them. "Mother" was gingerly holding an odd little bundle which I later learned contained various foreign objects she had found in our parents' bedroom. She asked for a match and kerosene oil. I found them and brought them to her. She selected a spot away from everything, dug a shallow hole, placed the bundle in, poured on the oil, lit it, and quickly moved away.

Phyl drew closer to me, and we watched the flames leap high, then die down to a smoldering mass. It gave off a strange, unpleasant odor, causing us to cover our noses. When it had burned to her satisfaction, "Mother" went and covered it with loose earth. She picked up a couple of sticks and laid them on top in the sign of the cross.

Phyl and I exchanged glances. But even a layman such as I had a good idea what that signified. Before she left, "Mother" informed us that she would return in two days to complete the sanctification.

"You are good people. I could feel it in your house," "Mother" said. "So, know that no evil shall ever overcome you."

We walked them to the gate. On our way back to the house, I began to wonder if Father had yet gone to see Mama as she had requested. I certainly did not want to meet him there. I wanted to change my mind and visit another day, but Phyl seemed so eager that I didn't want to let her down. We packed a basket with some of the groceries we'd bought the day before and added some of the eggs to it.

Mama wasn't expecting us, so when we popped in, she was pleasantly surprised.

Physically she looked great, but there was still that sadness in her eyes. I asked her if she had seen Father. She replied that she had, but did not elaborate.

Aunt Rose was busy outside sorting the herbs that she had gathered early that morning, so by mutual consent, we put off any discussion until she was able to join us. I hadn't noticed until then how out of place Mama looked in her present surroundings.

The cottage consisted of three rooms, not very large, two bedrooms and a living and dining room combination. One bedroom she used for her business. Aunt Rose had never married so she never did see the necessity of making additions.

I had no idea what Mama's plans were. But this was an arrangement that could last only temporarily. Besides, she was not the kind of mother who would walk out on her family, not when she wanted so much for us.

Aunt Rose spread the herbs on a large rack to dry and came in, wiping sweat from her face with a large handkerchief.

"Phew!" She grabbed a chair and sat down heavily on it. "Hot day."

Phyl and I agreed. It hadn't been easy toting that basket over between us.

After she had cooled off, Aunt Rose stared balefully at us, demanding to know the news we brought.

"Why do you think we have any special news, Aunt Rose?" Phyl hedged.

"Jus' know. Ah can feel it," she said "Besides, wat else would bring de two of you here dis time a day in dat boilin' sun, when you all know your mother in good han's?"

We looked at Mama, who nodded in agreement. I sat back and let my sister do the talking.

She told of the drama of the night before and the events of the morning without being interrupted. I looked keenly at Mama from time to time to gauge her reaction, but she merely adopted that tight-lipped look.

Yell, scream, say something! Stop being such a martyr! I pleaded in my mind. But nothing happened. She just sat there not saying a word. Why was this woman so apathetic? God... it was abnormal. I felt like screaming in frustration.

Phyl had stopped talking. Aunt Rose was bobbing her head knowingly, a smug smile on her face.

"Well, Ah guess it all over now," she addressed Mama. "Eh, Liz?"

"It will never be over." Mama said bitterly. "Nothing will ever be the same again because I won't ever be able to forget it."

I looked at her in awe. The depth of feeling by which she spoke belied my earlier assumptions.

"Then it's true about Mrs. Elliston?" Phyl asked.

"Oh, yes." Mama replied. "It was going on a long time. I was the last to know, and I would still be in ignorance if...." she broke off uncertainly.

"Mrs. Bowen didn't tell you...?" I dared to say.

She gave me a sharp look.

"How did you know that?" she demanded.

"It's just a guess," I said hesitantly. "Everything started to go wrong from the day she made that visit."

"True," Mama acknowledged nodding her head. "Now you all know why I hate gossip. It's a very destructive thing. Right or wrong, I always feel that what you don't know can't hurt you. But I suppose that whatever will be, will be. That day I listened to Hilda Bowen and what she said got to me. I confronted your father and he denied it. However, on the strength of what I was told, and against my better judgment, I went to see that woman. That Kessiah Elliston." Mama paused and gave a mirthless little laugh.

I thought, *what a horrible name for anyone to have and how well it suited her.*

"Of course," Mama continued. "She was as sweet as syrup. Denied everything Yet all the time, she had her plan to get me out of the way. Especially, as I understand it, she didn't think her husband was good enough for her anymore." Mama paused again, then said, "And I learned through 'Mother' Robinson that she may even have been trying to poison me, too."

"What!" Phyl and I gasped simultaneously. Then I remembered and I wasn't too surprised when Mama referred to the bottles of brew. Her lack of appetite and her refusal to have anything to eat forced on her had probably helped to save her life.

"My God!" Phyl said. "You know that for sure?"

"No, but why would she want to send me anything, I hardly knew the woman."

"Good question," I said, I was getting bolder by the minute. "An' why would Father bring anything from her to you in the first place?"

Everyone fell silent, considering the implication.

"I wonder if Father had any idea?" Phyl voiced her thoughts.

"Ah don't think so," Aunt Rose said thoughtfully. "Ah know your father an' he know Ah know him. He like to sow his wile oats, but he care a lot 'bout his family." She looked apologetically at her sister. "Sorry, Liz."

Mama just shrugged.

I suddenly saw the light. So that was the reason for the ongoing strife between them. I could clearly see how Father would resent Aunt Rose for having knowledge of his adulterous affairs. But why had she never told her sister what she knew, instead of keeping it all to herself?

That would always remain a puzzle to me.

"De truth is, as I see it," Aunt Rose continued. "That woman realize that she latch on to a good thing an' decide to get it all for herself. With you out de way, Liz, Ah have no doubt her husband would've been next to go."

"You know," Mama said with a sad look, "if it wasn't that he used such terrible means to get revenge, turning his wrath on my innocent children and destroying those beautiful animals, I could feel very sorry for him."

All three of us gaped at her. What an extraordinary woman! After all she'd been through, she still had feelings of compassion for someone who had hurt her.

I think it was at that moment that I lost all respect for my father, and my love for him was dangerously threatened. He had become just another man, one that I didn't even know. I guess I'd have to forgive him, but not now. Not now!

For weeks, our family had been at the mercy of an insanely jealous man scorned by a wife who had used some form of necromancy to terrorize our family in her attempt to get the man she wanted. Even if it meant killing for him. A crime that would undoubtedly go unpunished, for there would have been absolutely nothing to prove that one had been committed. And all because of a man of his age who could not contain his lust.

We talked a lot that afternoon. Mama opened up in a way I never thought possible. There were revelations that made me glad I knew nothing of them before. We told our mother all the things we'd kept hidden from her. She handled them all very well. But the thing that pleased me most was the fact that she had finally acknowledged that I was an adult.

She did not enlighten us as to when she would return home. No one tried to persuade her to make a decision. That was left strictly up to her. She made it quite clear that she expected us to carry on as usual, taking care of our father regardless of all that had happened.

Because, she explained, the problem was hers alone and she would handle it in her own way.

We were not allowed to take sides. That was my mother's way, and right or wrong, that's how it would be.

That evening. we had a very pleasant surprise. Father brought home a beautiful, healthy female Alsatian pup. I forgot everything in my eagerness to get acquainted with it.

"Now, don't spoil her." Father warned. I understood his concern. The pup was to be raised to be a watchdog. Floss sidled up to the new addition to the family and gave it a suspicious sniff, found it acceptable, and her motherly instinct kicked in.

Lester was kept on in the same capacity, and he made himself useful in other ways as well. In the next few days, I became fully aware of a noticeable change in the atmosphere around the house. The eerie, oppressive sensations that had plagued us had lifted. Everyone commented on it. It all seemed too easy. I kept expecting something to happen.

And something did happen that did not appear to have any relevance to the phenomenon of the past weeks.

It happened on the first night after "Mother" Robinson's second visit to our home. We were all preparing to settle in for the night when out of nowhere someone or something emitted a blood-curdling scream. It was drawn out and so full of agony that it sent goose pimples prickling all over my body. Paul, Andy, and little Janet were too stunned to speak or move. We listened but it was not repeated, which seemed rather strange.

We were not close enough to our neighbors to hear any sounds they would have made in their homes. Obviously, whatever made that sound would have had to be passing by. The sound was clearly a lament. But for what? I hoped the next day would bring an answer, but it was never explained and I ended up making my own deductions, which I never shared with anyone for fear of being ridiculed.

Father had now taken to coming home early and he would not go out again. It took some getting used to, but it was clearly a point in his favor. After two weeks had passed without further incident, I was ready to become a staunch believer in the power of spiritual healers.

A month slipped by and Mama was still with Aunt Rose. The inconvenience of her absence from home had put a strain on all of us, including her. The concern for her children's welfare finally prompted her to make a decision.

One morning, after everyone had left the house, I walked slowly and thoughtfully toward my parents' bedroom. I wanted to be sure that everything was in order. The door was closed, but I thought nothing of it. I opened it and was halfway in before I realized that someone was in the room. I let out a frightened scream and ran for the door.

"It's alright. It's only me." My father's voice stopped me.

"I ...didn't know you were in here," I blurted out, my heart pounding.

"Sorry, I decided to take the day off today."

"Oh."

"How's your mother?" he asked in a lifeless tone.

"She's fine, sir."

How many times had I said the same thing to him in the past days?

"When's she coming home?"

"I don't know, sir." The words were out before I could check them. Why had I lied to him? Maybe the imp in me wanted him to suffer as long as possible. I waited for him to respond, but he said no more. I started tidying up but I did not feel comfortable with him sitting there. I wanted to leave things as they were and wait for him to leave, but there wasn't time. I kept sneaking glances at him, but he simply ignored me. He just sat there, looking so drawn. He was obviously suffering great mental anguish. I felt no pity for him. Regardless of what Mama had said, I was still too full of resentment at his failure to take whatever action possible to help her... and of his treatment of me when I tried.

We had come so close to losing her. Just thinking of it made me want to cry. Perhaps it was wrong to feel the way I did about my mother, but the bond between us was so strong that it was as if she lived and breathed for me. That her life was my life and her demise would be mine also. My thoughts frightened me. I shuddered.

"Adelene?"

"Yes, sir?"

"Tell your mother I'm very sorry, and I miss her very much."

"Yes, sir," I hesitated. "But...but it would be better if you tell her yourself."

"I want to say the same thing to you, too." he went on as if he hadn't heard me.

"Me, sir?" I was surprised.

"Yes, I didn't understand." He did not move or look at me. "I mus' admit I was wrong."

Wonder of wonders! I never imagined I'd live to see the day he would humble himself enough to admit his faults. It got me thinking that whatever may or may not have occurred between him and Kessiah Elliston had obviously been of more importance to her than to him.

I believed his penitence was genuine. He could not have been that good an actor.

I relented somewhat. Maybe, despite the warning, I'd put in a good word for him.

Perhaps everyone really deserved a second chance. It was, after all, the Christian thing to do.

I left him sitting there.

EPILOGUE

Mama had wanted her return home to be a surprise for the younger children and had cautioned me not to let them know. James, Phyl, and I were the only ones privy to that knowledge. The one thing we hadn't counted on, though, was that Father for some obscure reason would have chosen that day to stay home, which was most unusual.

Despite that, I couldn't keep the smiles from breaking out on my face from time to time. My father at one point took notice and wanted to know what was making me so happy. I gave him a silly story about recalling a joke I'd recently heard. He gave me a curious look but merely grunted. Soon after, he got dressed and left the house, much to our relief.

Phyl and I, knowing in advance, had planned a surprise homecoming dinner to welcome our mother home. It would be a small affair with just our immediate family: James, his wife Anita and their young son Evan, Aunt Rose and at my insistence, Katherine.

Shortly after mid-day, we heard the rumble of James's car and I rushed out to help just as Mama was being assisted from the car. I grabbed a bag, James took another, and we escorted our mother into the house. We deposited the bags at her bedroom door just as Phyl hurried in from the kitchen to give Mama a warm welcoming hug, after which the latter began a tour of the house poking here and there until she felt satisfied. She then took me aside.

"Adelene, you've done a very good job," she said, giving me a little pat on the shoulder. "I'm proud of you."

I felt ten feet tall.

She then left us and went straight to her room, closed the door, and did not emerge for a long time.

Phyl and I were still busy preparing a special homecoming dinner we knew everyone would enjoy when our siblings walked in from school, all looking glum, having missed, I suppose, their daily visit with Mama at Aunt Rose's cottage. Janet was the first to spot her.

She emitted a gleeful scream and literally threw herself at our mother, wrapping her little arms tightly around her. The boys, less dramatic, moved at a more leisurely pace with wide grins on their faces as they, too, hugged their mother.

Me? I was so overwhelmed I teared up. So did Mama, and that for her was saying quite a lot. It was a moment we would always remember and cherish.

Much later, when Father returned, his reaction was no less dramatic when he saw Mama. He just stood and gaped at her.

"Liz," he gasped, and moved toward her.

"Albert," was Mama's crisp reply as she moved out of his reach.

"I didn't know you were coming home today," he gave me an accusing look. I didn't flinch, just looked innocently back at him. I guess he'd figured why I'd been so happy.

"Well, I'm here." Mama did not look at him.

"How...how're you feeling now?"

"Feeling fine. Thank you." There was no warmth in her tone.

Realizing there was not much to be gained at that point, he turned abruptly and went outside. I looked keenly at my mother and wondered what the future had in store for us becoming a happy family again. I walked across to the window and looked out.

Father was sitting on the stump of a mango tree that had snapped during a hurricane. Although his back was turned to me, I could tell by his posture that he was troubled. I quickly turned away when I found myself succumbing to pity for him. I looked at Mama. She had a smug smile on her face. I knew then that there was forgiveness, and time would take care of the rest.

We all had a wonderful time that evening. Mama gave a little speech about caring and honesty and the importance of such practices in one's everyday life. Father sat with his usual expressionless face. I tried not to look at him.

The succeeding days were spent in preparation for Phyl's wedding and plans for my future. It was decided that in order for me to fulfill my ambition it was necessary for me to leave home to attend a technical school to be trained in my chosen field. Leaving my mother would not be easy, but there was no other way.

Father? Well, I'm happy to say, had undergone a change for the better, which we all hoped would be permanent.

As to our ordeal, we would never solve the mystery as to how the terrifying things we had experienced were accomplished, but it was probably best not to dwell on them for the sake of our peace of mind.

ABOUT THE AUTHOR

Born and educated in Jamaica, West Indies, Iris Graham has seen a lot in her many years, and her childhood memories of family, friends, and neighbors are ever present and vibrant. She still recalls the fun times of family life in Jamaica—a strict upbringing laced with love and affection from a doting father and value-based mother. It was a simple but joyful life which remains etched within Iris. She realized at an early age that she had an innate gift for words and dreamed of becoming a writer. But life's challenges and other priorities got in the way of realizing her dream and, although never realized, she continued to capture her thoughts and remembrances on paper. She has come full circle now and is sharing her remarkable experiences with us, the reader. Today, Graham lives a modest and comfortable life in central Florida.